BLOOD TIES
IN
KEY WEST

BLOOD TIES

IN KEY WEST

Norah-Jean Perkin

Susan Haskell

ABSOLUTELY AMAZING eBOOKS

ABSOLUTELY AMAZING eBOOKS

Published by Whiz Bang LLC, 926 Truman Avenue, Key West, Florida 33040, USA

Blood Ties in Key West copyright © 2015 by Norah-Jean Perkin and Susan Haskell. Electronic compilation / print edition copyright © 2015 by Whiz Bang LLC.

All rights reserved. No part of this book may be reproduced, scanned, or transmitted in any form or by any means, electronic or mechanical, including photocopying, recording, or any information storage and retrieval system, without permission in writing from the publisher. Please do not participate in or encourage piracy of copyrighted materials in violation of the author's rights. Purchase only authorized ebook editions.

This is a work of fiction. Names, characters, places, and incidents either are the product of the author's imagination or are used fictitiously; and any resemblance to actual persons, living or dead, businesses, companies, events, or locales is entirely coincidental. While the authors have made every effort to provide accurate information at the time of publication, neither the publisher nor the authors assume any responsibility for errors or for changes that occur after publication. Further, the publisher does not have any control over and does not assume any responsibility for author or third-party websites or their contents.

ISBN 978-1-515108-62-7

For information contact:
Publisher@AbsolutelyAmazingEbooks.com

BLOOD TIES
IN KEY WEST

Chapter One

Despite the insistent bass pounding from the loudspeakers on either side of the stage, tonight only dust motes swooped and swerved over the dance floor. Tuesday through Saturday night, patrons had to jockey for position in the mass of bodies gyrating to the latest hits, but tonight Viva Zapata was eerily quiet. Only the tables along the front windows were full, and one couple was sitting outside watching the always-entertaining Duval Street life wander by.

Melissa Saunders adjusted her headset and leaned her long, slim frame back against the thick wood that topped the bar. Only three people, all men, had staked stools at the enormous curved counter, their hunched shoulders and downcast eyes indicating their desire to be left alone with their beer.

Which was just fine by Mel. She'd had more than enough of patrons who couldn't get it through their thick skulls that she worked here, and no, she couldn't have even one drink.

The clink of glasses nearby drew her attention. She turned her head to see Becky set down a loaded tray of empty bottles and glasses. At five foot one, the golden-haired waitress was as petite as Mel was tall, a chubby-faced cherub whose good nature infused every word and gesture. While other staff members had been slow to accept Mel as one of the club's two bouncers, Becky had made her feel like part of the family from the moment she'd walked through the door two weeks ago.

Mel smiled at her co-worker, then nodded at the deserted dance floor. "Is it always this quiet on Mondays?" She'd worked Tuesday to Saturday the past two weeks, and the place had been packed every night.

"Yes, thank God. I need at least one slow night a week." Becky winked at her and hailed the bartender. "Gord, I need two Coors Light and a coffee. The strongest café cubano you've got, please."

She removed the glasses and bottles from her tray and stacked them near the sink behind the bar. "Even when we had live entertainment on Mondays, it was still quiet. That's why Damien doesn't bother any more and we just play Pirate Radio shows."

Idly, Mel wondered when she would meet Damien Flores. She'd seen the club's owner only once, but his dark, good looks and quiet, assured command of his staff had piqued her interest. According to other wait staff, he had only reluctantly quit his job as a Key West cop to take the reins of the family businesses after his father died eighteen months ago. Damien left the force to take over running the cantina business and left the running of the club to manager and friend Ryan Ronson. It was Ryan, a childhood buddy of Mel's brother, who had ignored the naysayers and hired her as a bouncer.

As she moved around the different rooms Mel let her gaze roam the sparsely populated tables, stopping at the movie poster advertising the 1952 John Steinbeck screenplay, *Viva Zapata!* She wondered how many rounds of drinks it had taken to name the bar after a spaghetti western.

As Mel watched, a slim but well-endowed blonde in a skimpy camisole top and matching chiffon skirt extricated herself from one of the tables and stood up. She said something to her companion, an oddly familiar dark-haired man in a knock-off Tommy Bahama shirt. Whatever she said, he wasn't impressed, and threw back half another beer under her angry glare. The blonde turned and stomped off towards the washrooms.

The crackle of static from Mel's headset distracted her from the floor and she fiddled with the controls. The volume lowered, she responded. "Yes? Ryan?"

"How's everything in there? Quiet enough you can relieve me at the front? Sippin's Vanilla Latte is calling and I'm too weak to resist."

"Sure, boss." Mel smiled. She got a kick out of calling Ryan boss. Hard to believe her brother's friend – the same boy she had traded punches with in the streets of Bahama Village – had a good, responsible job. And that she reported to him. "Be there in a second."

"I'm leaving now. Won't be long." She heard the click as he turned off his headset. Slowly she edged over to the wide front doors. She didn't particularly like checking out people as they came in, but it was a quiet night. How hard could it -- ?

A scream rent the air, then breaking glass and the clatter of a tray hitting the floor. Becky shrieked in pain and her hands flew to her face. Coffee ran down her neck and over her white satin tank top. The dark-haired man slouched back in his chair, only the saucer of the coffee cup sitting in front of him.

Mel tore off her headset and sprang across the floor. Before the man could move, she grabbed the collar of his shirt, twisted his arm behind his back and yanked him out of his chair. "What the hell d'ya think you're doing, bozo?"

The man was big, well over six feet tall, but he was also very drunk and didn't have the wherewithal to free himself. "Don' wan' coffee," he slurred. "That bitch gave me coffee."

"That bitch is my friend." Mel tightened her grip. Gord had vaulted over the bar with a cloth and a pitcher of cold water and was already bathing her friend's red face and watering eyes. It was impossible to tell how badly she'd been burned.

Rage welled up inside Mel. She fought the urge to give the guy a pummeling he'd never forget. Instead, she twisted his arm harder and shoved him towards the back door exit. This time he tried to fight back, planting his feet and wrenching sideways. Mel barely managed to keep them both upright. "Keep moving," she hissed. "You're out of here, *now*."

Susan Haskell

"D'you know who I am?" he demanded, his alcohol-laced breath polluting the air around them.

"No, and I don't care." She gave him another vicious shove.

"You can't put me out . . . I –"

"I can and I will."

She wrestled the door open just past the base of the grand double staircase that lead to the rumored second floor bordello rooms, pushed the door open wider with her hip and shoved him out into the back parking lot. He yelped in pain as he toppled to his knees on the uneven brick courtyard, damp with March drizzle. Dark shadows reared overhead from the mesclun-shaped foliage along the fence.

She made sure the door closed and locked before leaving. No way he was getting back inside. As she pulled it shut, he struggled to his feet. He looked back, then lunged for the disappearing opening.

His fingers grasped the edge of the door and Mel grabbed the handle to force it shut.

Three loud bangs followed one after the other, like the backfiring of a car. With each bang, the man's body jerked. His fingers slid from the handle and he crumpled to the ground.

***

The hiss of the zipper closing the body bag was a familiar sound to Damien Flores. As a former homicide detective with the Key West Police Department, he'd heard it plenty of times before. He'd just never realized how loud – and how final – it sounded. But then, until now, the body inside the bag had always belonged to a stranger.

Not to someone he knew. Not to Tony.

He stood stiffly to one side as the attendants hoisted the bag into the back of the medical examiner's truck, slammed shut the doors, climbed into the cab and drove away, all seemingly in slow motion. As the truck disappeared, taking the body of his younger brother and only sibling to the morgue, he finally noticed the water that had been seeping under the collar of his shirt, courtesy of the warm drizzle that had been falling since before he'd arrived at the club.

A light touch on his arm made him turn. Dan Matthews, his former partner, loomed behind him. The light shone off his shaven, polished head and the uncompromising features that had earned him the nickname Kojak and been used to frighten more than one suspect into blurting out the sordid truth. No smile softened those harsh features now, but Damien saw the unspoken compassion in his friend's pale blue eyes.

"We're finished now," Dan said. "You need to go home, get some sleep. If you think of anything else that might help us find Tony's killer – anything at all – call me - anytime."

Damien nodded. The two men shook hands, and Dan lumbered off to his car. The odds of finding Tony's killer weren't good, and they both knew it. Murders around bars were notoriously hard to solve. It was late, dark, and there were no witnesses, or at least none that hadn't melted into the night before the police cruisers screamed up to the scene.

Even when murders occurred inside bars packed with people, it had always been difficult to find even one witness who would admit to having seen who had pulled the trigger or used a knife. Apathy, dislike of cops, fear of retribution, just passing through as a tourist – whatever the reason, most bar-goers passed on co-operation and feigned blindness and deafness.

But Damien didn't plan on letting any of that prevent him from finding the murderer. No one killed his brother and got away with it. Not as long as he was alive.

The last of the cruisers disappeared from in front of the club. Gone were all the people milling about the parking lot dotted by a few tables that ran along the side of the club where the filled-in pool used to be. Damien glanced at his watch. Four-thirty a.m. According to police, his brother had been shot shortly after eleven-thirty, five minutes before Damien arrived, and thirty minutes after he should have been there.

On leaden legs, he walked up and down Duval a couple blocks, seeing only Ryan's one-of-a-kind red convertible. As a believer in climate change, Ryan had lovingly built the hemp-bodied kit, but it also got him a lot of dates.

The street had only a few stumbling tourists who had closed down other Duval bars open 'til four am. Tony and Cristina must have come by cab, their preferred mode of transportation since the BMW had been repossessed. Had Cristina gone home? He hoped so. Tony's wife's pitiful sobs had felt like stabs to his heart, each one a bloody reminder of his broken promises.

Guilt flooded over him and his hands balled into fists at his side. Time enough later to deal with what should have been. He turned around and headed back to the front doors.

Inside, he blinked. Instead of the usual comforting darkness, punctuated by a few strategically placed colored lights over the bar, along the walls and embedded in the dance floor, the place was ablaze with light. Every fixture had been turned on, including some he'd never noticed before. In the blinding light, permeated by the yeasty smell of flat beer, stale cigarette smoke and strong coffee, the place looked stark and desolate.

Damien had appreciated the stories surrounding his new venture. Viva Zapata was rumored to once have been a popular bordello and speakeasy and of course, haunted. Its cavernous property once featured an unused full-scale swimming pool with a huge fountain. After being boarded up for over fifteen years, it had been renovated, but retained its old style Key West open air bar so was one of the premier attractions on the famous 'Duval Crawl.'

He assumed he was alone with his thoughts. Then he saw the two figures sitting at a round table on the far side of the dance floor. He recognized one -- his manager and security chief -- immediately. The bright light made Ryan's artificially blond hair look lighter than ever, and gleamed off the muscular arms below the sleeves of the black t-shirt stretched across his well-built chest.

His lips tightened. If Ryan had been there, doing his job, then maybe none of this would have happened. For a moment he allowed his irritation to flare, then abruptly killed it. He was being unreasonable. Hell, if *he* had been on time...

His train of thought derailed as his gaze fell on the second person at the table, a striking young woman he'd never seen before. He looked again and frowned.

If Ryan had hired her as a waitress, he'd made a big mistake. Young and attractive, yes, but everything about her screamed attitude, from her defiant slouch to the dark eyes narrowed on him with a disturbing mix of hostility and wariness. Spiked, burgundy-tinted hair had been raked away from an impossibly pale face with the high cheekbones and full lips that could have belonged to a model. But not the arms. Bared by a sleeveless, black, form-fitting top, her arms were sleek and strong and looked capable of holding their own in any street fight.

With a start, he connected the dots. She was strong enough to throw his brother out of the club... that meant –

A sudden motion across the room caught his attention. Cristina stood in the entranceway to the corridor leading to the washrooms. She'd clearly repaired some of the ravages caused by her tears, but he'd never seen the sharp-tongued blonde look so fragile. Her face was bare except for a few streaks of old makeup and puffy eyes from crying, her white-blonde, shoulder-length hair greasy and disheveled, her camisole and skirt creased and stained beyond repair. Worst of all was the wan, lost look on her face.

Their eyes met, and the composure she had clearly just regained crumbled. A low cry, like that of a wounded animal, emitted from her throat. She staggered towards Ryan and the dark-haired woman.

Damien launched himself across the room to support her, but before he got there her moan turned into a shriek. Her shoulders stiffened, her eyes blazed, and she pointed accusingly at the woman sitting beside Ryan.

Susan Haskell

"There she is. There's the scumbag who killed my husband."

Then she flung herself at the bouncer.

Chapter Two

The attack caught Mel off guard. Pain shot through her scalp as Cristina grabbed a handful of hair and yanked. She raked her nails across Mel's left cheek, then started punching.

Mel pulled out of Cristina's grasp and raised one arm to fend off the blows. No way she was going to raise a hand to the woman who already blamed her for her husband's murder. But that didn't mean she'd sit here and take her abuse.

The blows stopped as quickly as they'd begun. Mel lowered her arm. Club owner Damien Flores had dragged Cristina away from her and was struggling to hang onto his writhing, screeching sister-in-law. Despite his powerful build and over six-foot height, it was like trying to hold on to a stick of butter.

"Let go of me," Cristina shrieked, kicking and flailing at him. "Let me at her. She killed Tony. It's all her fault."

Mel stiffened at the accusations. They were off base, a product of the woman's grief and outrage over her husband's death, and she knew she should ignore them. But it was hard, even though she knew she'd throw the guy out again in a flash. She hadn't wanted Tony Flores dead. Bounced, yes. In jail, sure. But shot dead right in front of her? *No way.*

Ryan squeezed her shoulder and handed her the blue bandanna that had been tied around his upper arm. "Here, you're bleeding."

Mel raised her fingers and felt the sticky blood congealing on her cheek. She pressed the cloth to it and raised grateful eyes to Ryan. "Thanks. I didn't —"

"She deserves to bleed," Cristina interrupted. She fought to escape Damien, but he continued to hold her back despite the kicks and jabs she aimed at him.

With a final shake, he pinned her arms to her sides and held her back against him. "Stop it, Cristina," he said firmly. "You're tired and upset. You need to go home."

Though he spoke to Cristina, his dark, bleak eyes glared at Mel with a coldness she found hard to ignore. A coldness that made her feel far more terrible than the worst of Cristina's accusations. It took everything she had not to flinch away from that look.

But his words – and his continuing steel grip – had the desired effect on Cristina. Her chest heaved under the flimsy top and she still glared at Mel and Ryan, but at least she had stopped shrieking and fighting to get at them.

After a moment, Damien loosened his grip. With a gentleness that startled Mel, he lifted his big hands to Cristina's narrow shoulders and stroked her bare arms. "It's okay," he murmured over and over again, as if he were soothing a small child. Mel couldn't drag her eyes away; she'd never seen a man touch a woman with such gentleness.

Cristina shut her eyes and exhaled, and Mel sagged against the back of the chair. *Thank God. No more –*

Suddenly Cristina's eyes flashed open. Her face contorted with hatred and she flung Damien's hands off her arms and turned on him. "Why are you taking her side?"

The expression on his face remained calm, though the lines bracketing his mouth deepened. "I'm not taking anyone's side," he continued in that same soothing tone. "She didn't pull the trigger, any more than you did. She just . . ."

He didn't finish. Instead, he reached for Cristina. "It's late. Let me take you home."

"I don't want to go home. Not with you." She backed away, her eyes blazing again, her fair skin flushed with anger. "Where were you, anyway? If you'd been here on time, none of this would have happened. You're as responsible for Tony's death as *she* is."

Damien blanched, and Mel was shocked to see the guilt that flashed across his face before he regained control. Even

Ryan who had been sitting very still through the ordeal looked uncomfortable.

Damien tried to reason with Cristina again. "This is not the time to figure out what happened. Not when you're so upset. Let me take you home and we can –"

Cristina tossed her head, whipping her bottle-blond locks around her head. She crossed her arms. "I want Ryan to take me home."

Damien paused. He looked at Ryan and nodded slightly. Ryan sprang to his feet and came over and took Cristina's elbow. "C'mon Cristina. Let's go." He glanced at Damien. "You'll lock up?"

He nodded. Ryan turned, and after a final nod to Mel, escorted Cristina out. Mel pressed the bandana to her cheek and pinched her lips together. There went her ride. She felt inside her pocket for her cell phone but it was gone.

Silence settled over the club. Mel glanced at Damien. He hadn't moved since Ryan and Cristina left. A deep frown was fixed on his handsome face; he seemed to have forgotten she was there.

She stood up; the scrape of her chair on the pitted wooden floor echoed through the empty room. The noise jolted him from whatever faraway place he'd gone, and he blinked at her.

"I'll be going now, Mr. Flores," she said. She looked away from his stricken gaze and started for the phone behind the bar to call a taxi.

She'd made it about half way when he spoke. "No, wait."

She stopped but didn't turn around. So this was it, then. She should have known it was coming from the look on his face the moment he'd realized that she was the one who'd thrown his brother to his death. The police detective, the big bald guy with the tough cop demeanor, had insinuated more than once that she had been in on the murder somehow. She shouldn't be surprised that the dead man's brother thought so too. Cristina certainly did.

She squared her shoulders and slowly turned to face the inevitable. She raised her chin and threw out the challenge.

Susan Haskell

"So I guess this is the part when you fire me, huh?"

~ ~ ~

Damien blinked. The fact that the woman's words came so close to mirroring his intentions knocked him off balance. He knew she was the bouncer who had thrown Tony to his killer. But what followed next, he wasn't sure.

She lifted her chin a notch higher. Her cat-green eyes narrowed with the same defiance he had noted earlier. Her long, slim body dressed in form-fitting black top and tight black spandex jeans tensed in preparation for . . . for what? Did she think he was going to attack her the way Cristina had?

Something deep inside him flared at her challenge and the unspoken accusation behind it – that he believed her responsible for Tony's death. The accusation grated, more so because it had been his immediate, irrational response the moment he'd seen her sitting at that table with Ryan. But he wasn't Cristina, and he wasn't irrational.

He clenched his fists and clamped down on his careening emotions. He ignored her question. "Do you need a lift home?"

It has her turn to blink. Surprise, then suspicion flickered across her face, a face, he realized, that didn't look anywhere near as tough as he'd first thought in the club's harsh lighting. In fact, her features, with the dark brows, straight nose, high cheekbones and wide mouth, could as easily be described as exotic. Only the bloody slash across her left cheek made her look dangerous. The fists clenched at her side relaxed and the bandana dropped to the floor.

"I – uh . . . it's okay. I can get home by myself."

He swooped to retrieve the bandanna. When he arose to hand it to her, he was close enough to see the pulse hammering in her muscular neck, the agitated rise and fall of her chest.

"Where do you live?" he demanded.

"White and Petronia."

The cross streets, of a middle class residential area not far from his own, surprised him. He'd expected her to rhyme off one of the Key West Housing Authority apartments. Nothing about her suggested anything the least bit middle class.

"Help me turn off the lights and I'll lock up."

He turned on his heel and headed for the main light panel. He heard her head for the bar and the switches behind the counter. One by one the lights went out, until the club was plunged into darkness with the exception of filtered light from the clerestory windows behind the bar. Damien headed for the entrance of the club and waited while the woman gathered her purse from behind the bar.

Slinging it onto her shoulder, she countered him again. "I'll call a taxi."

He headed to the door, opened it and motioned her through. He set the alarm, then followed her out. "Never mind. It's easier to take you home than worry about you standing here on the sidewalk waiting for a cab. You're only a couple of minutes out of my way."

When she didn't argue, he was relieved. He headed for his Infiniti, parked in front of the Grand Vin Wine Bar. It had been the closest he could get to the club after Tony's murder. The woman kept pace with him, her long legs effortlessly matching his stride, but she made no effort to converse. Thank God.

He unlocked the passenger door and automatically held it open. She gave him an odd look, but got in, gracefully sliding her length into the comfortable space. He slammed the door shut and went around to his own side.

Neither of them spoke as he started the car and headed up Duval to Truman. He occasionally glanced at her in the uncomfortable silence. Her face was expressionless, and she leaned away from him and looked out the window as if she were alone. The bandana lay still in her lap, wrapped around one hand.

It occurred to him suddenly that he knew nothing about her except that she'd bounced Tony from Viva Zapata to his death. "What's your name?" he demanded abruptly.

She didn't move. "Mel Saunders."

"Mel?"

"It's Melissa, actually. Melissa Saunders."

Damien frowned. Something about the name bothered him. "Is there a reason your name would be familiar to me?" he asked.

She shrugged. "How should I know?"

Her flip answer irritated him but he pressed on. "Well, Me-li-ssa." He drew out the syllables of her name. He really needed to get home to bed. "How long have you worked for me?"

She yawned. "Two weeks."

"Ryan hired you?"

"Yeah."

He grimaced. Melissa Saunders, whoever she was, wasn't the talkative type. At least not at five in the morning. Which made two of them. But there were a few things he needed to know.

"Where'd you work before?"

"Russian Delights."

He swore. "That dive?"

"Yeah. That dive."

"Why'd you leave?"

For a long moment she didn't answer. Finally she twisted towards him, the bandana crunched up in one hand. "Look, we don't need to talk. The police already interrogated me."

"These aren't police questions," he said flatly. "These are employer-employee questions, and I have every right to ask them. Now, why'd you leave?"

She eyed him sullenly, but after a moment mumbled a response. "It was too rough. Too many knifings, too many attempted robberies, too many people getting hurt, too many cops, too many –"

As abruptly as she'd begun, she stopped. But he knew what she was going to say. *Too many deaths.* He grimaced. *Yeah, so she'd come to Viva Zapata to get away from it all. And brought it with her.*

His stomach tightened but he persevered. "How long have you been a bouncer?"

"A year and a half."

"What did you do before that?"

"I was a waitress."

He studied her out of the corner of one eye. "A waitress, huh?"

"Yeah." She paused, then startled him with the first bit of voluntary information. "I wasn't very good."

Now why didn't that surprise him? "Why'd you become a bouncer?"

"I hit a customer with a tray when he kept pulling me into his lap. Instead of sacking me, the manager offered me a job as a bouncer."

Damien suppressed a snort. "So have you had some training in self-defense, security, that kind of thing?"

She sounded more defensive than ever. "A little. I've taken self-defense courses at the Keys Community College, and I'm working on my black belt in Taekwondo. I have first aid and CPR from the Red Cross, too."

Fat lot of good that did, Damien almost muttered aloud. He gripped the steering wheel harder. He was being unfair. His brother had died, but she was the one who had seen him shot and killed only inches away from her – and seconds after she had tossed him out the door. Unless she was made of stone, she had to be hurting, maybe even be in shock.

As he stopped at the light at White Street, he furtively glanced at her again. For the first time he noticed the dark smudges under her eyes. The black slash of dried blood across her cheek stood in dark contrast to her deathly pale skin. A twinge of guilt assailed him.

"How old are you?" he asked quietly.

"What? Oh. Twenty-five."

It surprised him a little, though he knew it shouldn't. Ryan was only twenty-eight. So was Tony. Or at least, he had been.

The reminder of Tony brought a spurt of pain to his temples. Grimly he returned to her challenge at the club. "Tell me why you think I'm going to fire you."

She jerked her head around to look at him, her expression incredulous. "Oh, come on. It's obvious."

When he didn't say anything, those amazing green eyes narrowed. "You used to be a cop. You probably still think like one. And the one who interviewed me, you know, the bald guy, he kept asking if I knew someone was waiting outside to kill Tony."

"And did you?"

"Of course not!" She glared at him "How could I? Your brother threw hot coffee in Becky's face so I bounced him. That's all. Maybe I shouldn't have, but it's too late to second guess now."

The outburst was the first sign that Tony's death had rattled her. But she was also right. All the staff and customers interviewed agreed on what had happened. Tony had provoked the incident by throwing scalding coffee in Becky's face. There was no way something like that could have been planned or foreseen, and he knew Becky sure as hell wouldn't have volunteered for it.

Still, he found it difficult to erase his doubts. The spark of recognition her name prompted bothered him, too. *Why couldn't he remember?*

On the other hand, maybe his suspicions were only the result of the human need to blame someone, anyone, for what had happened. Or maybe, he thought more darkly, it was an attempt to take the guilt he felt and unload it onto someone else. "Did you know he was my brother?"

She shook her head. "Not then. I thought he looked familiar, but it was only afterwards I realized why. The second night I worked the club you came in for a few minutes." She surveyed him slowly. "You look a lot alike.

Damien pondered that one as he pulled up in front of a small and tidy shotgun cottage, typical in the Meadows area. There were several mature orchid trees casting shadows across the well-tended garden between the sidewalk and the freshly painted decorative spindles of the porch. He stopped the car and looked at her. "You own this?"

"No. We rent the guest cottage at the back of the property. It used to be a pottery studio in the 70s. It's a little dated but fine for us."

"Us?"

She didn't bite, so his curiosity about the existence of a Mr. Bouncer remained unsatisfied. He waited for her to open the door and get out, but she didn't move.

Instead, she straightened, took a deep breath, and turned a now somber face to him. "I'm sorry about your brother, Mr. Flores. I really am."

Her gaze was softer, mistier than before, and somehow he knew she meant it.

He cleared his suddenly thick throat. "It's Damien," he said quietly. "Call me Damien."

She opened the door and started to get out, then turned back. She looked at him. "So are you firing me, or not?"

The bubble of closeness popped. His chest tightened under a renewed flood of suspicion and doubt. God, he wanted to fire her. The words were on the tip of his tongue.

Instead, he looked at her hard. "That depends."

She hesitated only a heartbeat. "On what?"

His gaze bored into hers and his fingers tightened on the wheel. "On what the police investigation turns up."

Chapter Three

"Local Bouncer Implicated in Club Murder."

Mel gasped at the bold headline that screamed from the front page of Friday's *Key West Citizen*. It could only refer to her.

Gritting her teeth, she flattened the paper out on the coffee table and read on. Where the daily crime report on Wednesday had merely referred to a shooting death with no leads outside Viva Zapata, today's story featured an interview with the grieving widow and her take on what had happened. The story omitted any mention of Becky's face being scalded, referring only to a scuffle that had resulted in Tony Flores's ejection. It identified him as the former manager of the club, something Mel had learned only after his death. Damien Flores had assumed control when Tony had left to enter a drug rehabilitation program last year.

"Tony had turned his life around. He was ready to come back as manager. If that bouncer had only done her job right, my husband wouldn't be dead now."

The damning quote from Cristina made Mel's stomach churn. The queasiness intensified when the next paragraph identified her by name, and said she was one of a growing number of female bouncers in Key West and Stock Island. The story went on to say that police refused to comment about whether or not she was a suspect.

Suddenly a chubby baby hand grabbed a fistful of newsprint and yanked. As the flimsy paper crumpled and tore, a grin of delight spread across the ten-month-old's round face.

"No, Kirsten, no." Mel nabbed Kirsten by the wrist, and gently pulled the paper from her sticky fingers. Once the child had learned to crawl, she'd been into everything. Now that she could pull herself up to cruise beside the furniture, it was even worse.

Mel pushed the paper aside and picked her up. She pointed to the paper. "No, Kirsten, no. Don't touch."

She brushed her lips over the child's dark brown curls and inhaled her sweet scent. It was impossible to be angry with the blue-eyed imp, but she had to learn there were some things she couldn't do or touch.

Kirsten in her arms, Mel stood up. It had been only three months since her younger sister's violent death had left the baby alone and without parents. Determined that the little girl would never suffer the abandonment her mother and aunt had endured, Mel had stepped into the breach and managed to gain custody. Now she couldn't imagine life without her.

But what if she lost her job? Damien Flores hadn't fired her yet, but after this front-page news story, it was only a matter of time. Unfair or not, it wouldn't be the first time a bouncer was made the scapegoat. And the Department of Children and Families had made it clear when she became Kirsten's legal guardian that the girl would be removed if Mel failed to provide a stable, secure home life for her. If she didn't have a job, she couldn't provide that kind of life.

"I hate to tell you, but Kirsten has just thrown up on the back of your dress."

Mel whirled about at the sound of her roommate's voice. Joanie waddled into the kitchen from the second of the cottage's two alcoves used as small bedrooms. At twenty, the pixie-faced young woman looked sixteen, a fact made all the more jarring by the bulge of pregnancy accentuated by her tight lemon-colored t-shirt and navy short shorts. If what she said was true, she was about six months along with Mel's brother's baby. Mel tended to believe her. Why else would she have shown up, distraught, at their sister's funeral, clearly hoping Kevin would be there too?

But Kevin's baby or not, it didn't matter. Without Joanie as a roommate, Mel might never have gained custody of Kirsten. It had been a perfect solution; Joanie got room and board and a small salary and Mel got the live-in babysitter she needed to work nights. And once Joanie had accepted her pregnancy, and the fact that Kevin had disappeared, she'd regained some of the bounce that Kevin's desertion had sucked out of her.

Mel put Kirsten on the floor and twisted to look at the back of the black sheath dress she'd donned for Tony Flores's funeral. A beige blob of cereal now stuck to the dress just below her left shoulder blade. She grabbed a wet cloth from the sink and handed it to Joanie. "Want to wipe that off for me?"

Joanie took the cloth and started dabbing at the blob. Kirsten crawled back to the coffee table and pulled herself up again. With a mischievous look at Mel, she reached for the folded newspaper once more.

"You little rascal!" Mel snatched up the paper before Kirsten could get it, then set it on the kitchen counter. She needed those Keyswide Classifieds to look for a job later today.

Joanie resumed her dabbing. "When are Ryan and Becky picking you up for the funeral?"

"In twenty minutes."

Joanie made a face. "Why are you going? Especially after what the guy did to Becky."

Mel shrugged. "Because it's the right thing to do."

Joanie sniffed. "He's a loser, just like your brother. You told me to forget about losers like Kevin. I don't see why you don't do the same thing."

She finished the job, threw the cloth into the sink, and lumbered over to the couch beside the coffee table Kirsten was doggedly circling for the second time.

Mel grabbed the newspaper again and sat down at the kitchen table. In many ways, Joanie was right. Tony Flores was a loser. *Had* been a loser. But that didn't change the fact that he had paid for his attack on Becky with his life. That she had seen him killed right before her eyes.

Or that his brother was likely to fire the woman who had bounced him to his death.

Susan Haskell

The thought was not reassuring. Which was why she'd better take advantage of every minute to herself to search the want ads for a new job.

She shuffled to the back of the newspaper for the classifieds. The section with the murder story fell to the floor and she shuddered. *Was it too much to hope that club owners didn't pay attention to the newspaper?*

~ ~ ~

The Tony Flores eulogized at the funeral mass at St. Mary Star of the Sea bore no resemblance to the mean, surly drunk Mel had bounced Monday night.

A round, diminutive woman with grey hair, who turned out to be Damien and Tony's Aunt Liliana spoke lovingly about how the boys arrived in Key West in the 1980 waterborne escape from Fidel Castro's Cuba, the *Mariel Boatlift*. Their entrepreneurial father immediately started *Latin Lovers*, a chain of cantinas favored by Cubans living in the Florida Keys. Tears streaming down her face, she recalled in glowing detail the childhood and youth of the younger of the two Flores brothers, her Spanish accent growing thicker and thicker the longer she spoke. She praised *mi angelito Alberto*, the talented musician and artist who had won the hearts of all those around him with his charm and good nature. The accolades continued when a swarthy man in a black tailored suit and purple tie took the pulpit. With his overlong brown hair, deep set eyes and thick drooping mustache, he made Mel think of a young bloodhound.

She nudged Ryan who opened his eyes and looked up at the pulpit after she gave him an enquiring look. "That's Alonzo Salva," he whispered. "He's been Tony's friend since kindergarten. He's a lawyer, and now works for Damien and the club."

Salva, his gaze somber, spoke of Tony and him growing up in the tight knit *'Cayo Hueso'* Cuban community by Southernmost Point. Life was very good in the Upper Duval neighborhood of Key West that included Cristina and several other close friends, their own little brat pack. A muscle in Salva's jaw twitched when he spoke of how excited Tony had been when his late father had branched out from the Cuban cantina business, purchased Viva Zapata, and appointed Tony manager to get it up and running after being shuttered for so long. It was an area where Tony had excelled, injecting what started as an old decrepit, boarded up building with an excitement and creativity that had made it one of *the* places to see and be seen in Key West.

For what must have been the tenth time, Mel glanced over at the first pew, where Tony's widow Cristina sat beside Damien Flores. Mel had an unobstructed view of the back of Damien's neatly trimmed head, his broad shoulders straight and stiff under the expensive navy suit and white shirt. For the most part, he and Cristina had sat unmoving, but now Cristina's head fell forward and her shoulders began to shake with silent sobs. Damien slipped his arm around her shoulders and pulled her closer.

Salva's intense voice faltered and cracked. He paused, then cleared his throat and recalled how broken-hearted Tony had been when his mama had temporarily removed him as manager of Viva Zapata.

"Tony was well on the way to defeating his demons," Salva continued, his voice rising, his dark eyes focused on the front pew where Cristina and Damien sat huddled together. "He was about to return to work, and the club that he loved, when his life was so cruelly ended, cheating him and his family of all that he had to give."

With a dramatic flair, he paused and looked around the packed church, then back at the front pew. "What is particularly sad is that he never had the chance to resolve the differences that had arisen between himself and the older brother he had always loved and respected. He'll never have that chance now, and we'll all be the worse for it."

The comment struck Mel as particularly odd and tactless. Her gaze swiveled back to Damien. Was it her imagination, or had the owner of Viva Zapata just flinched? Was he stiffer than he'd been a moment before? Maybe, maybe not. As she watched, he removed his arm from

Cristina's shoulders, pulled it close to his side, and sat up even straighter.

~~~

Afterwards, at the reception in the church hall amidst the chatter and laughter, the *café con leche*, Cuban sandwiches and *Torticas de Moron* cookies, Ryan confirmed that Tony had normally been a personable guy. Even Becky, her cheek blistered and red from the coffee Tony had thrown at her, insisted his attack was completely out of character. She'd never seen him raise his voice, much less get belligerent, in all the time he ran the club, or in the months following his dismissal.

"What about the comment that Salva guy made? You know, the tacky one suggesting there was bad blood between Tony and Damien? What was that all about?"

Ryan brushed a hair off the sleeve of his too-tight navy suit. "I wouldn't exactly call it bad blood. It's no secret that Damien and Tony never got along, not even as children. Things just got worse when their father died. The old lady fired Tony and convinced Damien to leave the police department to run the family businesses. When she died a couple of months ago, Tony thought he was back in, but it didn't happen."

"Why not?"

"Old Lady Flores euchred him again. She left everything to Damien. Her will stipulated Damien could give Viva Zapata to Tony only after he'd been two years drug-free. The buzz is that on her deathbed she made Damien promise to stick to that schedule and to look out for *his little brother Alberto.*"

Mel shuddered. Perhaps the lack of a will after her sister's death wasn't such a bad thing after all.

"That's what Damien and Tony were supposed to be meeting about Monday night. Damien expected Tony to deliver an ultimatum: Give him the club now or he'd contest the will."

Mel glanced at Becky and frowned. In some ways it was a relief to know that all had not been well at Viva Zapata even before she'd come along.

Becky squeezed Mel's arm. "Come on. Let's pay our respects to Damien and Cristina."

"No."

Ryan straightened the off-the-rack suit jacket that just didn't fit properly over his bodybuilder's muscles and shoulders. "Come on, Mel. Stop blaming yourself. No one –"

"I don't blame myself." Mel pulled away from Becky. It was true. While she was sorry Tony had died, she knew she wasn't at fault.

She looked over at the people lined up to speak to Damien and Cristina, who were by a table on the far side of the room. "I just think it's better if I keep a low profile."

Ryan started to object, then stopped. He nodded to Becky. "Maybe she's right. Come on." He looked back at Mel. "We'll meet you back over by those great cookies."

Mel made her way through the large crowd of strangers to the table. Besides bartender Gord, in his flowered shirt and cargo shorts, and a few of the wait staff from Viva Zapata, she didn't know anyone there. Which was just fine with her. She could use a few minutes alone, sipping coffee away from the inquiring glances of her co-workers, glances that telegraphed their unspoken questions. *How are you holding up? How does it feel to see a man murdered before your eyes? Don't you feel terrible? Don't blame yourself.* The more people told her not to blame herself, the more she had the feeling that they actually thought she *should* be blaming herself.

As she poured herself a *café con leche*, she glanced around the room much as she would do at work. Despite herself, her gaze kept sliding back to Damien. He stood beside a round table on the far side of the room, while Cristina sat. A long line of mourners stretched out before each of them. Even with his suit jacket discarded, Damien looked more handsome and powerful than ever, but the strain of the last few days showed in the haunted look in his eyes, the lines around his mouth and the rare terse smile. Still, he spent several moments with each friend, relative or employee who came to show their respects.

For a moment she wished that she, too, could offer her condolences. But then, during a brief lull in the line, Damien looked around the room. His gaze flickered past her, and then returned. Shock and anger flashed across his face.

She turned away. Better than anyone, she knew how it felt to lose a sibling to violence. But Damien didn't want to hear that from her. He wanted her out of there. Or better yet, to admit to murder and give herself up to the police.

She raised the cup to her lips when a voice beside her ear said, "So you're the bouncer, huh?"

Her hand jerked and the coffee spilled, hitting her dress dead center. An unsmiling man in a wilted grey suit stood at her side. Though he couldn't be more than thirty, he had the look of a man who was born old. Of medium height, his blond hair was buzz cut and a slight paunch protruded over his narrow belt. Only his eyes were memorable, ice blue fringed with pale lashes, eyes that assessed her with biting clarity.

She swiped at her dress with a napkin, then straightened so her eyes were level with his. "I'm *a* bouncer. Who are you?"

"Esteban Maduro." He handed her a card. The card said he was a lawyer, with the firm Cabrera, Ramos and Maduro. "I'm one of Tony's friends."

Mel glanced from the card back to him. "Yeah?"

She handed it back, but he wouldn't take it. He nodded to the table where Damien and Cristina were receiving condolences. "Flores is pretty smart. But you can tell him for me, it's not gonna work."

"I don't know what you're talking about."

"Of course you don't." He smirked. "Just tell him that Tony's death changes nothing. We're still coming after him for the club."

~ ~ ~

Blood Ties in Key West

Led by the Castillo and Thurston hearse, the funeral procession snaked its way from Saint Mary's through the Old Town streets turning into Passover Lane, the main road into the Key West Cemetery. The nineteen acres on Solares Hill were the final resting place for tens of thousands of Bahamians, Cubans, sailors, Key Westers rich and poor, young and old, Salt Water Conchs and Fresh Water Conchs, all religions. There were only two kinds of live creatures here: huge iguanas that loved sunning themselves on cracked and sinking crypts, scampering off when a human passed by, and crowing roosters and hens, often with a brood of little ones following more or less in a straight line behind their mother.

A short line of cars continued slowly down Palm Avenue towards the Catholic section fronted by Frances Street. Graves were marked with everything from fortress-like mausoleums to tiny unreadable stones to modest headstones guarded by blank-eyed stone angels that Mel found oddly unnerving. Darla – or at least Darla's ashes – was buried too, but in an urn, in a box, in the farthest reaches of Mel's makeshift bedroom closet. No blank-eyed angels for her.

By the time Ryan found a parking spot out on the street and walked down Palm Avenue, the ceremony at the family plot had begun. The day was very hot for early March, and the unseasonal humidity for which Key West summers are famous had everyone drenched in their funeral finest. Sweat stung their eyes. The priest who had celebrated the funeral mass recited prayers in Spanish and English, with occasional weak responses from the crowd. Mel wasn't sure which family members even understood Spanish anymore.

From where they stood on the fringes, Mel could just see Damien. He stood ramrod straight, several feet apart from everyone else, his strained features frozen in a grim expression, his hands clenched at his sides. Despite herself, Mel felt a fleeting moment of pity. He'd lost his father, mother, and now his brother, in the space of two short years. From all accounts they'd been a close, if not always, happy family. She wouldn't know what that was like, but she could imagine.

A few feet away stood Cristina and another man. It was Esteban Maduro -- the jerk who'd forced his card on Mel and given her that disturbing message for Damien. She fingered the card in her pocket. She should have told him what he could do with it.

Now Maduro had his arm around Cristina's waist, as if he feared she might fall down. With her pale skin and platinum blonde hair, shrouded in black linen and lace, she certainly *looked* fragile. Mel touched the scratch on her cheek, evidence to the contrary.

The priest signaled the pallbearers and the coffin was placed into the above ground crypt. The priest gave the final blessing, then hugged Cristina and shook Damien's hand.

Damien took Cristina's arm and they headed for the funeral home's black limo. The other mourners drifted towards their cars parked in and outside the cemetery wherever they had been lucky enough to find a spot.

Ryan dug in the pocket of his shorts. He handed Becky his car keys. "Mel and I need to ask Damien if he wants any special arrangements for tonight." The club had been closed since Tony's death, but was reopening tonight with a popular band that had been booked months ago to help raise money for several charities. There was always some cause the locals were supporting with a fundraiser. In a town crazy about live music, a great band was always a draw and this was one of the last events before the snowbirds headed north for the summer.

Ryan grabbed Mel's arm. "We'd better hurry. I want to catch him before he gets in the limo." He took off at a jog, and Mel followed, the heels of her jeweled flip flops clattering on the uneven pavement. Car engines and scooters rumbled to life around them as the mourners prepared to leave. A whine that sounded like the buzz of a chainsaw came from the left of them. The buzz grew to a thunderous roar. Suddenly a helmeted driver on a scooter burst through the

Frances Street gate, landing with a crash amongst the remaining mourners, who scattered like frightened birds.

The driver pulled a pistol from his jacket and accelerated towards the limo.

Mel and Ryan leapt for Damien and Cristina just as the staccato sound of gunfire blasted through the air.

Chapter Four

Mel slammed into Damien with enough force to knock them both to the ground. Despite one-hundred-and-ninety pounds of male between her and the pavement, the impact jarred every bone in her body and cracked her jaw against his shoulder blade. Screams and dust filled the air, and the sound of the scooter's engine hit a deafening crescendo then receded as the driver took off down Margaret.

Mel tried to shield Damien from any further shots but he pushed her off and into the space between his body and the limo's back tires. She grabbed his shoulder. "Dami–"

"Lie still," he hissed. He shook off her hand as the dust and commotion began to subside and sat up. She struggled to a sitting position and looked around too. The biker was gone. The mourners, who had fled to their cars when the shooting started, began to stream back curious to see what had just transpired. His police revolver drawn, Damien's friend the Kojak-clone detective came running from the direction the shooter had disappeared. A couple of feet away, Ryan still lay draped over Cristina.

Damien knelt up and offered a hand to Mel. She took it, but as he pulled her to her feet, she gasped. Blood stained the collar of his shirt and dripped from his jaw. "Were you hit?"

He followed her shocked gaze, then touched his chin. "I'm okay. Must have cut it when I hit the pavement."

A groan nearby caught their attention. Beneath Ryan's still body, Cristina was shifting and trying to get up. *Why wasn't Ryan moving?*

Mel and Damien looked at each other, then dropped to the ground. Mel touched Ryan's shoulder. "Ryan?"

Warm hands grasped her upper arms and gently moved her aside. "I think he's been hit," said Damien. "Just before he tackled Cristina."

Slowly and carefully, Damien turned Ryan over, freeing Cristina from his heavy weight. The ill-fitting suit jacket flopped open, revealing a sickly-red bloodstain spreading across his chest.

Fear seized Mel. Oblivious to everything but Ryan, she pushed her way next to him and leaned over to listen for his breathing. Nothing. Nothing at all. In disbelief, she yanked off her jacket and pressed it to the gaping wound on the left side of his chest. Ryan couldn't die. Not Ryan. He'd always been so kind, willing to take a chance with her; he got her the job at Viva Zapata. He'd been more of a big brother than her blood brother. She looked up at Damien. "Call 911. Now."

But Damien already had his cell out and was barking orders into it. His dark eyes met hers. "An ambulance is on the way."

A man dropped to his knees beside them. Dully, Mel noted that it was the Kojak-clone. Damien jerked his head from Ryan back to Kojak. "It doesn't look good," he said. Mel gripped Ryan's limp hand, encouraged by its warmth that there might still be hope.

Kojak gestured to his car. "Uniformed units are on the way to streets in the area. There's a good chance we'll catch the shooter if he tries to leave Key West. An ambulance should be here in a minute or two."

A squeal of outrage came from behind Mel. Cristina, dazed and dirty, had just sat up and noticed Mel hovering over Ryan. "What are you doing here, you mur-"

Her gaze fell on Ryan's still form. The hand holding the black lace mantilla that had fallen off her head started to shake. "Ryan? . . . Ryan . . . What's wrong with him?"

Without warning, Cristina lunged at Mel. "Get away from him, you bitch . . ."

Damien inserted himself between the two women. "Hey, Cristina. It's okay. It's okay. She didn't do anything to Ryan. She and Ryan saved our lives."

Like two steel bands, his arms encircled Cristina, preventing the crying woman from lashing out at Mel, once again. Holding her, he struggled to his feet.

Kojak stood too. He instructed the mourners to stay where they were and that he would start taking statements in a few minutes.

Sirens sounded in the distance and gradually grew louder. Mel continued to press her jacket against the hole in Ryan's chest, but her hope faltered as she felt the warmth fading from the hand she gripped so tightly in her own.

Becky knelt down beside her. "Is he going to be okay?"

Mel couldn't answer. Her mouth, her mind, her lips, nothing worked. The two of them knelt in silence beside Ryan, holding silent vigil.

Finally the paramedics arrived. With gentle efficiency, they moved the two women away from Ryan, loaded him onto a stretcher, and carried him to the ambulance. No one said the words, "He's dead," but they didn't need to.

Mel had no idea how long she stood there, gazing after the departed ambulance, her bloodied jacket gripped in her hand, Becky at her side. She felt numb, from the inside out, and nothing seemed to matter, nothing at all.

"If you're all right, I have a few questions."

Mel turned in the direction of the voice. Kojak. Only this time all the pre-judgment, all the cynicism, had been wiped from his face. "Just tell me in your own words what happened."

She tried, she really tried, but everything came out in stilted phrases and half-sentences. The noise. The scooter appearing out of nowhere. The gun. The lunge for Damien and Cristina. And then . . .

Her throat closed and refused to work any more.

"Did you recognize the driver of the scooter? See a license plate number or even a partial?"

Mel blinked. If she'd noticed anything, it was gone. The color of the scooter or driver's helmet, his clothes, the license plate – it was all gone.

She swallowed and shook her head. "I'm sorry. No."

"What made you think the shooter was going for Damien or Cristina?"

She shook her head again. "I don't know. It just – well, who else could it have been by the limo?"

"Was there anything about the guy that made you think of Tony Flores's death?"

"No. I mean yes. Maybe."

She frowned. The roar of the scooter bothered her because . . . because . . . and then she knew.

"I think I heard a scooter start up after Tony was shot. Or at least it sounded like a scooter. With all the commotion after his death, it didn't seem important."

"Not important?" Kojak's eyes narrowed, his voice incredulous. "What about Ryan? Could the shooter have been after Ryan? Somebody who had it in for him?"

Dumbfounded, she stared at the detective. "I . . . I don't know."

"Hmm." Kojak stepped back. He pulled a card from his pocket and held it out to her. "If you think of anything, call me."

"Is there anything else you wanted to ask me?" The deep voice at Mel's side made her jump. It was Damien. She turned and looked at him but he was addressing the detective. "Cristina's in the limo. I'm taking her home now."

Kojak shook his head. "Tell Mrs. Flores I'll be around to see her later. You too. The medical examiner's report on your brother's death is in. I think you'll find it interesting."

Damien grunted his agreement, and Kojak headed to his car. Becky, who had sat down on the grass to gather herself, walked over slowly to stand beside Mel.

Damien's gaze met Mel's. For the first time since she'd met him, there was no trace of censure or anger in his manner, only that calm gentleness that so confounded her. Looking over at Becky he asked, "Are you all right?"

For a moment she couldn't speak. "Yes," said Becky with a sigh.

Damien's dark eyes narrowed as he surveyed them both. His gaze came to rest on Mel again. "I'm closing the club tonight. We'll open tomorrow. Can I count on you both to be there?"

Becky nodded vigorously. "Sure, Damien. Whatever you need."

When Mel didn't say anything, Damien frowned. "I'll be taking Ryan's job at the door. But I can't open the club without a bouncer. You'll be there?"

Mel nodded stiffly. "What time?" she croaked.

"Six sharp." He paused, and the strange warmth in his eyes made her throat grow tighter still. "I'm counting on you."

~ ~ ~

"Why didn't you tell me your brother was contesting your mother's will? I shouldn't have to find that out from your lawyer."

"My lawyer?" Damien scowled at his bald-headed friend. "You mean Alonzo? When were you talking to him?"

"I ran into him on the way in here. He was just leaving." Dan Matthews slumped back into the chair in Damien's office he'd taken only minutes before. "But that's not important. What's important is why you didn't tell me."

"Why would I?"

Dan shook his head. "You're gonna make me spell it out for you, aren't you?" He sighed. "Motive. It gives you motive to off your brother. Cristina, too, for that matter."

Damien stood up and leaned against the filing cabinet that held the club's personnel files. He'd come in early to make sure everything was ready for the club's busiest night of the week. And to review the personnel records and the list of individuals banned from the club, anything that might suggest a link to his brother's death.

He stared hard at Dan. "This is *me* you're talking about. Your former partner."

Dan held up his hand, palm forward. "Yeah, yeah. But I'm not talking about what we both know. I'm talking about how it *looks*. So far you're the only one we know about with a motive for killing Tony. There's nothing else to tie you to his death, and I don't expect there to be."

He paused, and his eyes met Damien's. "But I do expect you to be straight with me. Just as important, keep out of the investigation. I know you want to find your brother's killer, but you need to leave it to me. I mean it, Damien."

Damien neither nodded nor shook his head. Dan meant well, but nothing he said or did would prevent him from trying to find Tony's killer. It was the least he could do for his brother, for his family. The thought that he could be a suspect in his brother's death rankled, but it wouldn't stop him from conducting his own investigation.

He changed the subject. "What about Ryan's shooting? Got anything on that yet?"

"The lab is checking the bullet to see if it's from the same gun used to kill Tony. We've found a couple of casings, too. So far we've been working on the theory that your sister-in-law was the real target of yesterday's shooting. But I'm not so sure any more."

"No?"

"Two things. First, your brother's blood analysis shows a huge dose of cocaine, likely injected either just before or after his arrival at the club. That would account for his uncharacteristic belligerence, especially if he'd been off the drug for some time.

"And second, Cristina insists that if Tony got hold of cocaine, it had to be from Ryan. She said Tony stood and talked to Ryan at the door for several minutes after they arrived. And that Tony headed for the washroom as soon as he'd ordered a beer. She also says that when Tony was manager here, he and Ryan occasionally hung out together."

Damien mulled that one over. He wasn't surprised to learn that Tony had weakened and started using again. Users often had to hit rock bottom before they were able to throw off the addiction. *His* mother had hoped that the lure of regaining the club he loved would help Tony succeed. Clearly it hadn't.

But Ryan? When Tony managed the club, they had become fast friends. Once Tony had been kicked out, Ryan had worked diligently with Damien to clear the club of drug peddlers and lowlifes as their friendship grew too.

Blood Ties in Key West

"Have any of the staff mentioned anything about Ryan and drugs?" asked Dan. "What about that bouncer? She seemed pretty tight with him."

Damien frowned. An image of Mel formed in his mind, not the sullen, provocative bouncer with the chip on her shoulder he'd first met, but the young woman bent over Ryan's still form, holding his hand, speaking encouragingly and desperately clinging to hope that he continued to live. "Don't know."

"Is she here yet?"

Damien glanced at his watch. "Should be."

"Get her in here."

~ ~ ~

When Mel sauntered into his office a few moments later, Damien couldn't help but be impressed by her *cojones*. Everything about the leggy bouncer screamed bold assurance, from the black, form-fitting flares and sleeveless top that revealed her toned body and smooth, sleek arms to the aggressive tilt of her chin and the dark, spiked, henna-tinted hair. Even the scratch across her cheek, which should have made her look vulnerable, only enhanced the impression of a lethal, attractive weapon ready to take on all comers – including him and the police.

If she was putting on a show, it was a damn good one, and one he found disturbingly erotic. Like it or not, she pulled every one of his sexual strings, provoking desires and needs best ignored.

"Yes?" The one word, along with the narrowing of her cool green eyes and her hands-on-hips stance, communicated her irritation at being summoned. For an instant, Damien wanted to back her into a corner and rattle that confidence with a blistering kiss that would leave her breathless and wanting more.

Silently berating himself for the stupidity of *that* idea, Damien nodded at the second chair lined up in front of his teak desk, and then back at Mel. "Sit down. Detective Matthews wants to ask you a few questions about Ryan."

Her expression didn't change. "Thanks. I'll stand."

He shrugged. "Have it your way. Dan?"

Dan turned his chair to face Mel. "How long have you known Ryan Ronson?"

"As long as I can remember. When I was a kid, he was my older brother's best friend."

"So you grew up with him? Bahama Village?"

The mention of an area that many equated with drugs and violence jolted Damien. He stared at her, but she ignored him.

"I left when I was eleven. I hadn't seen Ryan for years until a few months ago when I met him at a funeral."

"A funeral?" Dan's voice sounded the surprise that Damien felt.

"My younger sister's funeral. He was there. That's how he knew I was a bouncer. When a job came up here, he offered it to me."

The mention of the job reminded Damien why he'd come in early. To examine the personnel files, including Mel's, as well as the bar's exclusion list. Dan had arrived before he'd had the chance. He opened the drawer of the filing cabinet now. Maybe there'd be something in her or Ryan's file that would help in the investigation. He found the right files, yanked them, and sat at the desk to look at them.

"Was Ryan your boyfriend?"

"No."

"What about drugs? Do you know whether he used or sold cocaine or any other drug?"

Mel's face darkened. She shook her head from side to side.

"Ms. Saunders." Dan adopted his most reasonable tone, part of his professional bag of interviewing tricks. "Ryan is dead. Whatever you say now can't hurt him . . ."

Mel frowned and her eyes glittered with suspicion. If she knew something, and that was a pretty big *if*, she wasn't going to bite. "As far as I know, he didn't use or sell drugs anywhere."

"So you never saw him sell drugs at the club?"

"No, never."

Blood Ties in Key West

Damien opened Mel's file, and scanned the contents. Her resume, and the application she'd filled out, corresponded to what she'd told him the night he drove her home, and what she was saying now. He read the education section and looked up at her in surprise.

"What about Tony Flores? Did Ryan give him drugs the night he died?" pressed Dan.

Mel glared at Damien, then looked back at Dan. "If he did, I didn't see it."

"Does it surprise you when I say we have witnesses who saw Ryan give Tony cocaine?"

Her expression wavered, and then stubbornly returned to the closed expression she had worn since entering the office. "I don't know."

Having found a weakness, Dan followed up with another provocative question. "What about you? What are you on?"

"I don't know what you mean."

"Come on, Ms. Saunders. We know where you grew up. We know your brother Kevin's been in the Monroe County Detention Center on drug charges."

"I don't use drugs."

Kevin Saunders! The connection Damien hadn't been able to make before finally clicked into place. He returned to the cabinet and rifled through the files until he found what he was looking for. Kevin Saunders.

He yanked the page and its accompanying photo out of the file and held it in front of Mel. "Is this your brother?"

"Where'd you get that?" She reached for the sheet but he pulled it back.

"Ryan didn't show you this?" he demanded.

"No."

"Well, he should have." Damien turned to Dan. "Kevin Saunders was one of the lowlifes banned from the club after I took over. Until then, he was selling drugs, even shooting guys up in the can."

"Hmm." Dan studied the picture. "D'you think he might have had it in for Tony?"

Damien frowned. "If he did, he waited a long time. Besides, it was Ryan and I who threw him out, not Tony. Shortly after that he was jailed for possession."

Dan took another long look at the picture and handed it back to Damien. He looked at Mel. "You don't look much like your brother."

"So?"

"To your knowledge, did your brother ever own a scooter or motorcycle?"

"I don't know."

Dan let it go. "Okay, back to yesterday at the cemetery. You and Ryan were jogging towards Cristina and Damien when the scooter passed through the gate. Why?"

"I told you yesterday. Ryan wanted to ask Damien a question about the club."

"What made you and Ryan tackle my friend here and his sister-in-law?"

"We saw the rider draw a gun. I can't speak for Ryan, but I assumed the guy was after Damien."

"What made you think that?"

Mel looked at Dan as if he were stupid. "I don't know about Ryan, but no one has any reason to kill me."

"Oh?" Dan raised his eyebrows. "And is there a reason to kill Mr. Flores here? Or his sister-in-law?"

For the first time since the interview began, she flushed. "His brother was killed last Monday. It's only natural to think..."

"It couldn't have been someone after Ryan? One of his drug connections? Your brother, pissed off that Ryan had ruined his business?"

She exhaled sharply. "If it is, I don't know anything about it."

Dan nodded abruptly. "Thank you, Ms. Saunders."

She eyed him suspiciously, then turned towards the door.

"Mel?"

Slowly she turned back to face Damien. Her gaze flicked to the sheet of paper in his hand, and she pressed her lips together. "Yes?"

Damien put down the sheet and picked up her personnel file from the desk. "Your application says you've taken criminology courses at the Florida Keys Community College."

"Yes."

"Why didn't you apply to the Key West Police Department? With your education, your height, and your training in self-defense and martial arts, you would have been a shoe-in."

"A cop?" She uttered 'cop' with the distaste usually reserved for the slimy stuff found under rocks. "I don't want to be a cop."

Damien and Dan exchanged looks.

"Can I go now?" she demanded.

"Detective Matthews is leaving. I'd like you to wait. We need to go over tonight's arrangements."

Dan stood up. "I'll be in touch. Try to have a quiet night, Flores."

As the door shut behind Dan, Damien waved Mel to sit down. She took the chair beside the one vacated by Dan.

Damien shoved aside the files and leaned forward. "I've got an old buddy coming in tonight to help me keep an eye on things. His name's Gustavo. He should be here any time.

"I want you to circulate inside and outside. Make regular rounds of the washrooms too. If you see or hear anything that could be linked to Tony or Ryan's deaths, let me know. And if you run into any trouble – if anything starts to get physical – call for backup. Gus or I'll come running."

Resentment clouded her face. After a moment of silence, she blurted out, "You don't think I can do the job, do you?"

His stomach tightened. Suddenly tired, he picked up the files, stood up and turned to the cabinet. *Let her think whatever she wanted.*

The cabinet door squealed in protest as he opened it. He heard her push the chair back and stand up.

Susan Haskell

"Is that everything?"

"Yes."

She made it as far as the door before she stopped and slid something out of her pants pocket. The motion drew his eyes to the enticing curve of her bottom, a sight that set off a slight stir in his groin that was the last thing he needed.

She returned to the desk and extended a manila business card to him. "Here."

The name on the card killed all thought of tantalizing curves. He scowled. Esteban Maduro. "Where'd you get this?"

"Yesterday, at the reception in the church hall. The guy gave me his card and told me to give you a message."

"A message?"

"Yeah. He said to tell you that Tony's death didn't change anything. They're still coming after you for the club."

Chapter Five

Damien's face darkened and his brows bunched together. He crumpled the card and dropped it to the floor. "Why were you talking to Maduro? You know him?"

Mel shook her head. "No. He came up to me at the reception. Asked if I worked at the bar." She didn't mention the way the jerk had actually phrased it; Damien didn't need to know about another person blaming her for his brother's death.

Damien kicked the crumpled card across the office defiantly. "Do you know what this is about?"

The black stretch t-shirt and khakis suggested polite society, but the look he shot her was pure jungle, steaming with fury and challenge.

If it was meant to intimidate her, it had the opposite effect. Her skin tingled with excitement, her pulse quickened, every cell in her body poised for combat. Just let him try to push her around.

"Your brother wanted the club back," she said flatly. "He was contesting your mother's will."

The fact she knew his business appeared to shock him. He started to respond, then shut his mouth abruptly. Weariness replaced the anger blazing from his dark-brown eyes, and the lines bracketing his mouth and fanning out from his eyes appeared deeper than ever. He worked his fingers at his sides. Finally he just waved her off and turned away.

His sudden shut down surprised her, but she shrugged it off and headed for the door. As she reached for the knob, she looked back. What she saw brought her up short. Damien was sitting now, his elbows on the desk, his head in his hands, a complete contrast to the angry man who had demanded answers from her only moments before. Clearly

Susan Haskell

the strain of the two deaths and the continuing investigation, coupled with his own legal problems, were getting to him.

Not sure why his suffering bothered her, she re-crossed the room and stopped in front of his desk. "Are you all right?"

He didn't answer or look up.

She pressed on. "Can I get you something from the bar? A coffee? Beer? Water?"

She shifted awkwardly. She had an inappropriate urge to comfort him. A touch, a hug, a kind word, she didn't know exactly what, but *something*.

She grimaced. From her, yeah, that would work. *Probably about as well as if I punched him in the head.*

The seconds passed and he continued to ignore her. Finally she sighed and headed for the door once more.

"No. Wait."

At the muffled voice, she turned. "Yes?"

Damien had raised his head. The weariness and sorrow had fled. His black eyes narrowed with renewed suspicion, and the set of his shoulders and jaw telegraphed both determination and the hardening of his views after a moment of weakness. "Come and sit down. We need to get a few things straight."

Uh-oh. Mel walked back and sank into the chair across from him.

Damien leaned forward, his dark gaze raking over her with unforgiving harshness. He spoke with an icy control that only underlined his fury.

"I'm not at all happy to have you here, especially after discovering that I kicked your drug dealer brother out of the club eighteen months ago.

"I don't like the fact that your brother knew Ryan, and probably Tony, too. I don't like the fact that Ryan hired you, and then the next thing I know, both he and Tony are dead. There are too many coincidences."

His expression grew grimmer. "If I had anything – anything at all – to pin on you, you'd be out the door right now. But for the moment, I need you."

He sat back in his chair. "Report to me every half hour tonight. And know I'll be watching you every minute. If I find out you're involved in any way, or you're withholding any information, you'll answer to me. Understand?"

"Yes." Seething with anger, Mel shot up from the chair. She should have known better than to waste her time on pity for him. Or expect thanks for saving his life at the cemetery.

Tossing her head, she turned and stalked to the door. If not for the fact she couldn't afford to lose another night's pay, she'd walk out of Viva Zapata right now and never come back.

~ ~ ~

It didn't take long for Damien to realize that watching Mel was a bad idea. A *really* bad idea. Because the more he watched the provocative bouncer, with her confident stride and taut curves clothed in form-fitting black, the more turned on he became.

Everything about her, from the tilt of her hennaed head to her confrontational, hands-on-hips stance, seemed designed to taunt and challenge him. Watching her was like waving a red flag in front of a bull, inciting Neanderthal urges he hadn't known he possessed. Hell, he wanted to conquer her, to tame her, to make her his in the way only a man could. And he didn't like her effect on him one bit.

Especially since she was the last woman in the world he should want. Even knowing she might be involved in his brother's death couldn't snuff out his fantasies, ignited anew each time he saw her swagger by. Instead, the allure of the forbidden made him hotter than ever.

He groaned, leaned back against the bar and tried to turn his attention to the full house. Despite four days being closed, Viva Zapata was back big time and packed with a Saturday night crowd intent on partying. People walking on Duval heard the music punctuated with the loud laughs of a happy crowd and were drawn in to check it out.

Damien attributed the crowd to the live band *Key Lime Pirates,* locals who had skyrocketed in popularity since they did Sound Check at the Green Parrot open-air bar and now were one of the hottest bands in Key West. There were lots of locals in the steamy house tonight, but in general the crowd was younger, fans of the group's up-tempo cover songs, as well as its male singer and guitarist.

Damien squinted through the smoke and flashing lights at the blond-haired singer beating his guitar and gyrating his hips a couple feet away from the mass of bodies dancing and writhing on the jammed dance floor. In his opinion, the guy's singing and playing were a plus, on top of the appeal of his rugged good looks and a stage presence the ladies seemed to love.

Damien scanned the dance floor, and then the rest of the packed room, but didn't see Mel anywhere. He'd be glad when tonight was over. He'd been on edge from the moment he walked through the door, a condition only made worse by a suspect bouncer and her relationship to a drug pusher who'd known his now dead brother.

"Hey."

He tensed at the now familiar smoky voice, but he didn't turn to look. Why in God's name had he insisted the woman report to him regularly?

"Everything's fine," Mel shouted over the music.

"No trouble in the washrooms?"

She pulled off her headset. "What?"

His headset already hung around his neck, but still he couldn't hear her. Automatically he moved closer, slipped one arm around her shoulders and yelled in the direction of her ear. "Any trouble in the washrooms?"

The moment he touched her bare arm, he knew he'd made a mistake. Her firm, smooth skin felt good under his fingers, too good. It was hard to resist exploring the warm, silky flesh, especially with the fresh scent of her hair and skin launching a second affront on his senses.

She shook her head. If she noticed his hand on her arm, she ignored it. "I think we're going to make it through the night without any real trouble."

"Good." He paused and leaned in closer still. "You've done a good job tonight."

"Yeah?" Her eyes narrowed.

"Yeah." Reluctantly he released her arm. As much as he hated to admit it, what he'd said was true. He'd watched her constantly, and from the start it had been clear that when it came to the job, she was professional all the way.

It was almost as if she had a sixth sense for trouble, homing in on the offending table or corner before things got out of hand. In the space of the first two hours, he'd seen her save a baby-faced bridal party woman from the persistent attentions of a foul-mouthed lout; turf a couple of smart-asses who thought they could get away with lighting up joints in a back corner; boot out a drunk and cut off a handful more nearing the danger point; and intervene in at least three arguments before they got nasty.

Only once did she touch a client, and that was to help the staggering drunk to the door and put him in a cab so he would get to his hotel safely. The rest of the time she relied on everything from diplomacy and motherly concern to sarcasm, wisecracks and blunt warnings. It didn't hurt that she was an attractive woman, but also one who looked like she was willing and ready to kick some serious butt.

He'd realized once and for all that she didn't need a minder when he saw her step between two glowering six-footers, one of whose shirt was soaked with the Dark and Stormy the other guy had spilled on him. By the time Damien made his way across the room to intervene, the two of them had backed off and sheepishly returned to their tables and their dates.

He was about to ask her what she'd said to them when hoots and laughter rose above the music blaring from the speakers. He glanced at the stage. A pink bra dangled from the neck of the lead singer's guitar. As he struggled to free it, a pair of pink panties flew through the air and hit him in the face. The dance floor exploded with laughter.

Damien sputtered and looked at Mel, but she was staring at the cramped stage, a frown creasing the bridge of her nose. He followed her gaze. A woman, naked except for a tiny black mini-skirt, had pursued her underwear onto the stage.

Susan Haskell

She raised her arms over her head, and thrust her pendulous breasts under the lead singer's nose. He smiled at her but continued playing like he'd been through this naughtiness before.

If it had ended there, Damien might have let it go. But the woman wanted her idol's attention. She draped her arms around his neck and flattened her body against him and his guitar. When he tried to shake her off, she hung on tighter, and wrapped one of her legs around one of his.

Automatically Damien started for the stage, only to be yanked back by the sleeve of his shirt. "That's my job," Mel said.

For a second he just stared at her, then nodded. It was what he paid her to do, after all.

In less than five seconds she had climbed onto the stage. Joyous tears rolled down the woman's face as she clung to the singer, who tried to continue playing and singing in between attempts to loosen her hold.

Mel touched the woman's shoulder and said something to her. The woman started hooting with delight as she tightened her grip on the singer. Mel yelled at the singer and he nodded. Then she grabbed the woman's arm and pressed on a pressure point near her collarbone.

The woman screamed and jumped back from the singer as if she'd been stung. Mel grabbed the woman's wrists, twisted her arms behind her back and pushed her towards the edge of the stage. They were almost there when both women crashed to the floor. The music died, replaced by jeers and catcalls.

Immediately Damien pushed his way through the crowd. When he reached the stage, Mel was kicking at the blue-haired moron who had tripped the two of them and still clung to her ankle. The bare-breasted woman punched and clawed at Mel while Gus tried to intervene.

Damien delivered a sharp blow to the male attacker's wrist. With a howl of pain, the guy let go of Mel's ankle. Damien grabbed him by the shoulders and yanked him back from the stage. As he whirled him around to march him to the nearest exit, the room plunged into darkness.

For a split second silence reigned. Then bedlam erupted, with screams and shouts, shoving and the pounding of feet on every side. The man in Damien's grip jerked suddenly, then gasped and sagged towards the floor. Damien struggled to keep him upright.

The emergency lights flickered on, their weak beams illuminating panic-stricken men and women tripping and falling over each other in their stampede for the doors.

Damien felt something sticky and wet on his right hand. He looked down at the blue-haired man and gasped. Blood, and plenty of it, oozed from a wound in the front of the man's right shoulder.

Chapter Six

It was all over in less than an hour. An ambulance and two police cruisers screamed up to the door within seconds of each other. Mel and Damien and Damien's buddy Gustavo did their best to corral the people who hadn't run out the exits as soon as the main lights failed. The paramedics bundled the stabbed man out to the waiting ambulance, while the police questioned and searched the patrons. Neither the lead singer nor Damien pressed charges against the bare-breasted woman whose attack set the whole mess off, though the police questioned her at length. It was her boyfriend who had been stabbed.

To Mel, the most troubling part was the lighting failure. Someone had deliberately cut off the power at the fuse box in the utility room, at the exact moment when the person with the knife had struck. And while the victim was the man who had sent her crashing to the floor with his girlfriend, it didn't make sense that he was the real target.

It had to be Damien. But no one asked her opinion, and because of the darkness, no one had seen anything. There was no weapon, no bloodstains at an exit, nothing.

Her right eye swelling shut and her arm scratched and sore from the woman's attack, Mel kept her head down as she went about her final checks at the club. Mercifully, no one paid any attention to her, not even the Kojak-clone when he arrived a few minutes after the uniformed officers. Speaking in low voices, Damien and his friend did a circuit of the bar, ancillary rooms and courtyard.

All the remaining partiers and most of the staff had been allowed to leave by the time Mel approached the bar, where Damien was deep in conversation with Dan Matthews. Her head hurt, her eye hurt, and she wanted to go home, but she felt duty-bound to point out to her employer what he and the police seem to have missed.

She cleared her throat. "Damien" she rasped. Then, more sharply, "Mr. Flores!"

"Yes!" The irritation on his face disappeared the moment he saw her. "What happened to you?"

She shrugged. "The naked lady landed a punch, that's all. I'm going home now, but I need to– "

Damien stood up. "Not until we do something about that eye." His gaze dropped to her arm. "And those scratches."

"I'm fine."

He grabbed her elbow and propelled her around the bar. "I'll talk to you later in the day," he called over his shoulder to Dan, who got up, waved and left.

"I've got ice at home," she protested as he filled a plastic bag with ice, wrapped it in a bar towel, and pressed it against her eye.

He lifted her hand up to hold the ice pack, then took her other arm. "Come with me."

A few seconds later they were in his office, and he was rifling through the filing cabinet. When he turned around, he had antiseptic and a roll of gauze in his hands. He set everything on the desk beside the chair where she sat. "Why didn't you say anything?"

She didn't grace his question with a reply. What for?

He returned a moment later with a wet cloth, and sat down beside her. His fingers, warm and firm, gripped her wrist as he wiped at the caked blood on her arm.

He picked up another cloth, doused it with alcohol, then pressed it to the scratches. Despite herself, she winced.

He looked up from his work, a faint smile on his lips. "She got you good. Is this your first shiner?"

"No." She refused to meet his concerned gaze. She knew how to react to his anger and accusations. Concern was something else. Why was he asking her such dumb questions anyway? It wasn't as if he liked her.

He set her arm down and went to work unwinding a long strip of gauze. When he'd cut it off, he grasped her upper arm but she pulled away.

"This isn't necessary. Besides, I didn't come to you for first aid. I came to tell you something."

"What?"

"Someone tried to kill you tonight, Damien. I'm sure of it. The lights going off and the stabbing are just too much of a coincidence."

Surprise flickered in his eyes. "Funny. That's what I thought. Dan, too." He frowned and looked at her hard. "But I wouldn't have thought you would notice – or care enough to tell me."

"Why do you think that?" she snapped. "Because I'm a murder suspect? Because my brother's an ex-con? Because I grew up in public housing? Is that it?"

He had the grace to flush. "Maybe I've been too quick to judge."

She glared at him from her one good eye. "Not maybe. You *have* been."

"Ouch." He winced, then pressed his lips together. It looked as if he was trying hard not to smile.

"Well then, the least I can do to make it up to you is to tend to your wounds." He picked up the gauze. "May I?"

His admission mollified her a little. She might as well let him finish the job. She held out her arm. "All right."

Damien went to work once more with the gentle efficiency that she'd found so alluring the first time she'd seen him. The warmth of his hands and their fluid, rhythmic motion as he wrapped the gauze around her arm soothed her agitation, at the same time as her awareness of him fueled another kind of tension, one she definitely didn't want. He was close enough that she could smell the tangy key lime scent of the shampoo he used on his thick, brown hair, and feel the heat of his body as he worked over her.

He glanced up at her from under incredibly thick black lashes, the dark pools of his eyes smoldering with an unsettling warmth. "I've been watching you all night," he said. "You're good."

She struggled to free herself from the spell of those eyes. "I could have told you that," she sniffed.

He smiled as the harshness fell away from his face. For the first time she could believe he was the thirty years Becky had said he was. And a hundred times more appealing than she would ever have suspected.

"So tell me your strategy," he said. "How'd you prevent all those fights without lifting a finger?"

It was impossible not to respond to his change of attitude. She put down the bag of ice she'd been holding against her eye. "I'll let you in on a secret. Especially in a place like this, with a better-raised clientele, it's always easier for a woman bouncer to stop a fight. I step between them and they get this `My Mom taught me not to hit girls' moment' – and that's all it takes."

"What about the guys you get to leave without roughing them up? I was watching. It looked like you were whispering sweet nothings in their ears."

"Sweet nothings?" Mel laughed. "Hardly. What I said was, 'You can walk out like a man, or you can show your friends that you can get the crap kicked out of you by a girl. Works every time."

He laughed and she couldn't help joining him even though it hurt her eye.

Slowly his expression became more serious, and as it did, his eyes darkened to the black of velvet, soft, inviting, and dangerously intriguing. Her pulse quickened and she felt shaky and tense.

"You know, I never thought I'd be saying this to a bouncer."

"Say what?"

He took her hand and his heated gaze searched her face, coming to rest on her lips. The breath caught in her throat, and her lips parted of their own accord.

"That even with a black eye, you're beautiful. Beautiful and very, very hot."

Then he dipped his head and his mouth slanted over hers, as naturally and as confidently as if he'd done it a hundred times before.

She could have pulled away. She could have pushed him back. She could have slapped his face.

But she didn't do any of those things. Instead, she shut her eyes, all her attention, all her energy, focused on the wonder of the caress of his lips. The perfect pressure of his warm lips on hers, the exquisite taste, the tenderness she would never have believed from him if she hadn't felt it.

And then she kissed him back. Slowly, unabashedly, with a passion that welled up from deep inside.

When she finally withdrew, her lips tingling, she smiled ruefully. "That wasn't a smart thing to do."

"I know." He squeezed the hand he still held and didn't look sorry at all. "But in self defense, may I point out that you did kiss me back."

"Of course. How else would I find out how a cop kissed?"

He laughed. "You mean ex-cop."

"Whatever."

His eyes narrowed. He stood up and pulled her to her feet, then released her hand. "So how was it?"

If she were smart, she'd tell him it was terrible, awful, even substandard. But it hadn't been any of those things, and they both knew it.

Still, she wasn't about to admit it. "Not bad." She paused, "For a cop."

~ ~ ~

The face that stared back at Mel from the mirror in her bedroom at ten Monday morning was not a pretty sight. Much of the swelling had gone down, but her right eyelid was a livid purple that made her look paler than ever, and the scratched cheek reminded her of yet another night she'd rather forget.

It was not a face that anyone in his right mind would call beautiful, and definitely not hot. Even more definitely, it was not the face she wanted to take to the job interview she'd lined up for four this afternoon. She –

The ringing of the phone in the kitchen shattered the little cottage's quiet. As Mel finger-combed her hair, she heard Joanie pick it up. Kirsten was already in the front cottage, with their elderly landlord and landlady. Mr. and Mrs. Rubenstein had shocked Mel from the start, first with their unlikely acceptance of her and Joanie as tenants, and then with their offer to babysit Kirsten every now and then. They fawned over her as if she were a grandchild every time they saw her, and this morning had been no exception.

Suddenly, there was a loud crash, like the sound of the receiver being slammed into its cradle. "Pervert!"

Mel hurried into the kitchen. "What was that?"

Joanie made a face. "Some mouth-breather. Eeww!"

The phone rang again. They both looked at it. "I'll get it," said Mel.

She smoothed out a wrinkle in her black sheath dress with one hand and reached for the phone with the other. "Hello?" she said sweetly.

Dead air met her greeting. She was about to hang up when she heard what sounded like someone clearing his throat. Then the breathing started, fast and raspy, as if he'd just run up ten flights of stairs. Or was trying to fake heavy breathing.

"Get a life," she snapped, then replaced the receiver in its cradle. Too bad she hadn't sprung for the extra ten dollars a month for caller I.D. on the old landline.

"The mouth-breather?"

"Yeah." Mel nodded and reached for her black jacket. With cold water and plenty of scrubbing she'd managed to get the blood out it. She wasn't crazy about wearing it again, but she had nothing else suitable to wear.

"Have you gotten any heavy breather calls before this?" she asked.

"No. This was the first." Joanie wrinkled her nose. "Kind of an odd time of day to call, don't you think?"

"I don't know." Mel glanced at the clock on the stove. "We'd better get going. I don't want to be late for Ryan's funeral."

Joanie nodded and picked up a tiny patent leather purse from the table. With her spaghetti-strapped black crepe dress, rhinestone-studded black sandals and shiny purse, she looked as if she were going to a cocktail party, not a funeral.

But Mel wasn't complaining. If Joanie wanted to attend the funeral of a guy she'd never even met, that was up to her. This was the happiest she'd looked since they'd moved here. Pregnancy had filled out her narrow face, but could it also finally be erasing her bitterness?

Mel hoped so, but she also suspected Joanie harbored a hope that Kevin might show up at his old friend's funeral. Highly unlikely, but who was she to burst her roommate's bubble?

~ ~ ~

Everything about Ryan's funeral made Mel feel bad. The trek back through the potholed streets of the old, rundown neighborhood. The square non-descript funeral home, with its peach stucco exterior, tattered awnings and rusted fire escape. The haggard face of Ryan's older sister Lorraine, a single mother who struggled to support her two little girls. The generic eulogy, full of useless platitudes, given by the same no-name minister who'd presided over Darla's funeral. Ryan deserved so much better.

It didn't help that Damien ignored her. Looking handsome but drawn in light grey pants and white linen shirt, he'd glanced her way with only the barest of acknowledgments as he'd walked to a row of seats with Cristina.

But what exactly had she expected? She wasn't dumb enough to think that a moment of concern and one ill-advised kiss in the wee hours of the night would change anything. The venomous glare that Cristina sent her way made it clear nothing had changed in that department either.

When the service ended, Mel and Joanie filed out to the strains of canned organ music. They headed over to the reception area. Joanie was already antsy, and had spent most of the service looking around the drab room to see if anyone new had come in. Mel planned to stay only long enough to give her condolences to Lorraine. Then they were out of there.

Susan Haskell

Mel made her way over to Lorraine while Joanie headed for the table with a few plates of sandwiches, cookies and an old rusty coffee urn. The plates were spread around the table to make it look like there was more than there was. As she waited in line to speak to Ryan's sister, Mel watched Damien and Cristina on the other side of the room. They stood in a corner with Alonzo Salva, talking.

Or at least, Cristina and Damien were talking, while Alonzo stood by, listening intently and sipping from a cup of coffee. Whatever Cristina was saying, she was vehement about it; she waved her hands in the air and pounded a fist into the palm of her other hand. Damien seemed to be the one asking questions, nodding or frowning in response to Cristina's comments.

The receiving line moved forward, and Mel hugged Lorraine. "I'm so sorry about Ryan," she said. "He was always so good to me."

"Yeah. He was good to everybody. He came by regularly and gave me money every month for the girls." Lorraine nodded at her daughters, dressed in their Sunday best and sitting quietly beside her at the table. "We're going to miss him."

After a few more minutes of stilted conversation, Mel said her goodbyes. As she walked away, she glanced over at the corner where Damien, Cristina and Alonzo had been standing.

With a shock, she realized that all three of them were staring in her direction. She stopped and looked around, but there was nothing else going on that could have attracted those intense stares. It had to be her. And while she looked pretty beat up, she doubted that was the reason they were looking at her like that.

Abruptly she turned to search for Joanie. She'd had enough of funerals, enough of suspicion. Joanie chose that moment to sidle up to her, a plate with several tiny sandwiches in her hand. "Do we have to stay much longer?" she asked between mouthfuls.

Mel shook her head. "We can leave as soon as I hit the washroom. You stay here and finish your sandwiches. I'll be back in a minute."

The slightly cooler air of the hallway was a relief after the stifling meeting hall. Mel followed the signs to the woman's washroom.

"Pssst."

One hand on the door, she looked in the direction of the noise.

At first she didn't recognize the ragged man who stepped from around the corner. Then she blinked. *It was Kevin.* He looked terrible. Always thin, now his six-foot form verged on skeletal, an emaciation even his dirty beige jacket and ragged jeans couldn't hide. A sparse, scraggly beard covered his thin face, and his hair was long and unkempt. Even his dark blue eyes, always his best feature, looked weak and watery.

"What are you doing here?"

"I'm sorry, Mellie. I'm so sorry about Ryan."

"Yeah, we all are." She frowned at him, her shock turning to anger. "You couldn't have gotten here for the service? And what about Darla's funeral? You couldn't come to that either?"

His gaze darted past her. "Is she here?"

"Who? You mean Joanie?"

He ignored her questions. Instead, he rooted around in the pockets of his jacket, unearthing a dirty mostly white stuffed toy. Mel recognized it instantly. It was *Chicken*, Joanie's stuffed pet from Webkinz. Joanie had moaned about its loss almost as much as she had about Kevin's disappearance.

Chicken was especially popular in Key West because it looked like a sweet and cuddly Silkie, a chicken who had likely been brought to the Caribbean on the Silk Route, and whose white fluffy plumage felt like silk. Silkies were also polydactyl, sporting a fifth toe, instead of the usual four. Key Westers were always quick to embrace the unusual.

"Where'd you get that?"

"Give it to Joanie." He shoved it at her, but she backed away.

"It's better if you give it to her yourself." Mel didn't care, but she knew Joanie would jump at the chance to see Kevin again.

"Just give it to her, will you?" He stuffed the grubby toy into her hand, shoved past her and stumbled to the back exit.

Thumps and shuffling echoed from the stairs, followed by a muffled protest and a couple of rank expletives.

Mel winced. It sounded like Kevin had crashed into someone on the way out.

A moment later, Damien rounded the corner, looking annoyed and brushing off his sleeve. His brow creased when he saw her. "Did you see who that was?"

She almost blurted Kevin's name out, but stopped at the last second. "Nope."

Something about her tone must have struck a false note. Damien paused and looked at her hard. "Was it your brother? Was it Kevin?"

She stilled. Why should she tell him? "I don't know wh—"

Damien didn't wait. He turned and bolted to the door after Kevin.

Chapter Seven

Her cheeks stuffed with ham and cheese sandwiches, Joanie pouted. She looked down at her half-full plate. "Can't I finish these before we leave?"

Mel grabbed a paper napkin off the table, dumped the remaining food into it, and stuffed the package in her shoulder bag on top of the white chicken she'd yet to show Joanie. "No. We have to go."

A hand at the small of Joanie's back, Mel propelled her towards the exit. She wanted to get them both out of here before Damien returned. Or worse, Damien *and* Kevin returned.

Too late! Damien barely avoided crashing into Joanie in the doorway. He stepped aside and started to apologize, then saw Mel.

His face, red from exertion, darkened. His hand shot out and clamped onto her arm. "You're in an awfully big hurry to leave," he said.

Mel raised her chin. "I have an interview."

"Oh?" His eyebrows rose a fraction. "A job interview?"

"Yes." She wasn't about to tell him anything else.

His unsmiling gaze moved from her to Joanie, flickering over her pregnant belly, girlish face and cheeks still stuffed with food. Mel felt his fingers tighten on her arm.

He nodded at Joanie. "Do you mind waiting while I speak to your friend in private?"

"No problema." Joanie cast a triumphant smirk Mel's way, then waddled back over to the food table.

"Come out into the hallway with me," Damien purred, but Mel wasn't fooled. The purr hid an unmistakable current of menace. Every cell in her body tensed to alert.

Outside the gathering room, Damien backed her into a distant corner, then released her arm. He stared at her with the coldness of an enemy stranger. The kiss, the shared moment, had clearly been nothing but a mistake, one he wouldn't repeat.

"Why did you lie about your brother?"

She refused to let him cow her. His size, his maleness, his power, none of it mattered. Knowing the streets and alleys of the old neighborhood, Kevin had easily eluded Damien. Mel straightened and looked him in the eye. "Why would I tell you? You've made it clear you think Kevin had something to do with your brother's murder. Hell, you've made it clear you think *I* had something to do with it. Well, think anything you want. I'm not going to help you try to pin murder on an innocent man."

His eyes narrowed. "So you think he's innocent, do you? That's a pretty strong statement for someone who says she doesn't even know where he lives."

"I don't." She straightened her shoulders. "Are you finished? I need to go now."

He made no move to step aside and let her pass. Instead, his lips curved upwards in an icy smile. How could those lips have felt so warm and inviting only thirty-six hours ago?

"Actually, you won't be able to make that interview this afternoon," he said. "You and I are taking a little trip up to Marathon to the Shooters N Scooters shop."

The words *scooter shop* raised the hairs on the back of Mel's neck. Ryan's killer had come flying into the cemetery at Tony's funeral on a scooter. And there had been the sound of a scooter starting up outside the club after Tony was shot. But what did that have to do with Kevin?

As if sensing her question, Damien continued. "A few minutes ago Cristina provided some very interesting information about your brother. Seems Kevin used to work at the SNS five or six years ago, before he started hanging out at Viva Zapata."

"So?" This was news to Mel, but she was damned if she'd let Damien see that.

"So Tony and Cristina used to like to go shooting there. More importantly, that's where they met your brother Kevin."

Blood Ties in Key West

And where your brother turned mine onto drugs. He didn't say it, but he might as well have. The accusation hung over Mel like a noose.

She grasped her shoulder bag. "Very interesting. But I've got that interview."

She tried to slip past him but he blocked her way. His dark eyes bored into her accusingly. "What? An interview is more important than proving your brother's innocence?"

~ ~ ~

Shooters N Scooters was in Marathon just across the Seven Mile Bridge. The sprawling two-story windowless structure housed a shooting range with several lanes and the outdoor pen had both well-used older model and newer model scooters. Owner Mark Grady was as scruffy and ill kempt as an old hippie, but talked about SNS with a father's pride as he puffed on an aromatic Cuban cigar. His grizzled head bobbed up and down in recognition when Damien showed him a picture of Kevin Saunders.

"Oh, yeah. Kevin used to work here, up until a couple of years ago. His jobs were to set the customers up for shooting and help make sure everything was going smooth in the range. Outside, he'd make sure the tourists knew how to ride the scooters safely. Too bad he got caught up in a drug bust and went to prison."

Grady pulled on his cigar and slowly and skillfully blew out a ring of smoke. He looked from Mel to Damien. "Why you folks looking for him anyway?"

"He's my brother," Mel piped up. "We've been out of touch for a long time and I need to find him."

"Yeah?" Grady regarded her skeptically.

Damien was surprised she'd spoken. In the one-hour drive out here, she hadn't said a word, though the silence had crackled with tension and animosity. As well as that underlying sexual attraction that never quite went away.

"Kevin is out of jail now," he said quietly. "Is he working here at all?"

Grady shook his head. "Nope. Came around a few months ago. Wanted his job back, but I couldn't do it."

"Why not?" Mel sounded calm, but the clenched hands at her sides gave her away.

"Hey, don't get upset, sweetheart." Grady looked as if he was about to reach out and pat Mel on the head, then reconsidered when he took another look at her battered face. "Looks like you've got enough problems already without digging up the past."

Without missing a beat he turned to Damien. "Places like this are always under the microscope. I try to keep it clean so the feds don't get on my case and I get good ratings on social media. Kevin was a good employee, but I couldn't have him sellin' drugs to the kids." Damien suspected the man's comment was more self-serving than an expression of his true feelings, but it didn't matter. He pressed on. "Did Kevin ever take the scooters out?"

Grady nodded vigorously, the cigar bobbing up and down from the corner of his mouth. "He could tear a strip off the best of them," he said admiringly. "We used to call him the 'Black Knight' he was such a good rider."

Damien glanced at Mel. With each new fact pointing to Kevin as a potential killer, she pressed her lips more tightly together. He felt a twinge of regret, but brushed it aside. She had her loyalties; he had his. And right now finding out who killed his brother – and was trying to kill him – was more important than anything else.

"What about shooting? Was Kevin a good shot?"

"Never had better. He was also a great instructor. With all the drug use, it's hard to believe he had such a good eye and steady hand, but he did. He was the best." Grady winked at Mel. "He always liked to help out the girls."

Through the office window, Damien saw a van towing a trailer with two scooters pull up. "What about break-ins?"

"Occasionally. Mostly in the summer months."

"Any lately?"

"Funny you should ask. We had a break in about ten days ago. Lost one of our late model Zumas. A beautiful black number."

Damien's heart speeded up. Could it be?

He looked at Mel. She'd gone deathly still.

Her brother or not, surely she was thinking the same thing he was: Could Kevin have stolen the scooter and then killed Tony *and* Ryan?

~ ~ ~

On the trip along the Overseas Highway back to Key West, Mel alternated between anger and indignation then despair and disbelief. One minute she wanted to pummel Damien for his self-righteous pursuit of Kevin, the next she wanted to beg his forgiveness for her tenuous relationship with a potential killer.

Shading her eyes from the sun, she glanced at the clock on the dash. Four fifteen. There went her interview.

Damien noticed her looking at the clock. "Want me to let you off somewhere downtown for that interview?"

She shrugged. "Doesn't matter. It was a dumb idea anyway. An upscale place like that, they'd take one look at my face and the fact that I'd worked at Russian Delights and it would be all over."

For a moment Damien said nothing. Sunglasses hid his eyes, and his tanned hands rested calmly on the steering wheel. "There's no reason for you to leave Viva Zapata," he said, without turning his gaze from the road ahead. "Despite my initial reaction, I'm sure you had nothing to do with Tony's death. And I *know* you didn't kill Ryan."

"Thanks for the vote of confidence."

His hands tightened on the wheel, the knuckles turning white. He pushed down his sunglasses and looked at her. "Why are you so pissed off at me? I'm sorry about your interview. But surely you're not upset because I'm trying to find Tony's killer? Whether it's your brother or not, you must want him to pay for what he's done."

Mel exhaled. He just didn't get it. "I'm not upset because you're trying to find your brother's killer," she said through gritted teeth.

She turned to him. "I'm upset because people like you – rich jerks like you who think they own the world – always think that people like me and my brother and sister are to blame for everything."

Now that she'd started, the words tumbled out faster and faster. "You and the police can't wait to pin the murder on Kevin or some other no-good drug dealer. It doesn't matter that Tony was a drug addict, that he invited Kevin and others like him to sell drugs from his club. It doesn't matter that he almost blinded Becky with scalding coffee. What matters is that his family – your family – has money, and everyone jumps to solve his murder.

"Well, no one jumped when my sister was beaten to death four months ago. And you want to know why? Because she was a no-good welfare mother, that's why. No one –"

Mel's voice cracked. Too late she clamped her mouth shut. She hadn't meant to say so much. She didn't want Damien's pity. She didn't want anyone's pity.

An uncomfortable silence settled over the car. Mel focused on the traffic around them, growing thicker as they came towards the triangle at North Roosevelt.

Finally Damien broke the silence. "I'm sorry about your sister." He paused. "Want to tell me about it?"

"No." But even as she said it, her anger seeped away. What was the point? He wouldn't understand. He certainly didn't care.

"So how is it you hardly ever saw your brother?"

The question took her by surprise; she found herself answering. "My younger sister and I were put in separate foster homes when I was eleven. Kevin stayed with my mother and her boyfriend of the month. I think he left home for good when he was around fourteen."

"Your mother still alive?"

"No. She's been dead for several years. Kept saying she'd get rid of the guy and bring us back home, but it never happened."

"I'm sorry."

"Don't be." Mel couldn't keep the bitterness out of her voice. "I lucked out. I had great foster parents. Darla and Kevin weren't so fortunate."

Damien turned the car onto Petronia and stopped in front of her house, where a mass of fuchsia blooms filled the yard with blazing color.

Mel gripped the door handle, her anger surging anew. "And you know what? I don't care what you think about me or what you think you've found out about Kevin. I don't believe that Kevin killed Tony or Ryan!"

She jumped out, slammed the door and ran down the red brick path to her cottage.

Chapter Eight

In the dim light of the club, Damien saw him first and swore under his breath. The last person he wanted to see tonight was *that* dirt bag.

Esteban Maduro stood in the main doorway to Viva Zapata and squinted into the darkness. He wore the light grey suit and lavender shirt he had likely worn to work today, but had removed the tie. At first Damien thought he was looking for friends, or waiting for a date. But when he pulled out a notebook and pen, glanced toward the bar and started writing, Damien knew why he was really here.

He sauntered closer to the lawyer, and planted his feet. "You're blocking the doorway, Maduro. Either come in or get out."

"Nice to see you too, Flores." Maduro dropped the pad to one side and sucked in his gut. "Actually, I was hoping you'd be here. I wanted to have a little heart-to-heart with you about our mutual interests."

"We don't have any mutual interests."

Maduro laughed, but the mirth didn't reach his ice blue eyes. "Always such a joker." He exhaled and let his paunch fall back over his belt. "You know we do. It would have been nice if you and your brother had worked things out on your own. But you didn't show, and he got blown away."

"So Tony's dead," snapped Damien. "What's your point?"

Maduro's smile was long and slow and unpleasant. "Cristina's still alive. And as her lawyer, I've told her that what should have been Tony's should now be hers."

Damien scowled. "She's got money. She and Tony got fifty per cent of mama's house just last month."

Maduro shook his head and looked at Damien as if he were a recalcitrant child. "Can you hear yourself? How greedy and selfish you sound? Have you no concern for your sister-in-law? Just because –"

Without warning Mel sidled between the two men. "Oh, Mr. Maduro, how nice to see you this evening." Her voice was high and sweet as saccharine, and didn't sound like her at all.

Damien stared at her, perplexed. When she'd come in this evening after their visit to SNS, she'd looked as if she'd sooner poke sharp sticks in his eyes than come near him. What was going on?

Now she was doing a credible imitation of the hostess with the mostest. She glanced politely from Damien to Maduro. "Can I get anything for either of you gentlemen? Would you like to be shown to a table, Mr. Maduro?"

She raised one eyebrow at Damien and jerked her head slightly towards the door, her meaning clear. Did he want her to throw Maduro out?

Still perplexed, he gave a small shake of his head, then looked at Maduro. "No, it's all right, Mel. I'll take care of Mr. Maduro myself."

With a bright smile for Maduro, Mel strolled away towards the bar. Damien couldn't keep his gaze from following the lithe figure dressed in her customary black, couldn't prevent the rush of interest and stirring in his groin as she swung her shapely hips back and forth with exaggerated swagger.

"Nice piece of ass for a bouncer. Where you picking up your staff these days? A private security company? Or an escort service?"

Damien turned on the smirking lawyer, his hands fisted at his side. What he'd give to wipe the smile off his self-satisfied face and make him retract that cheap shot. With an effort, he controlled himself. Maduro probably wanted Damien to hit him. The next thing he knew, he'd be faced with a multi-million dollar assault suit.

"Are you finished?"

"Not quite." Maduro opened his suit jacket and put the pad and pen away. When he closed the jacket, he looked up. "I know Tony was trying to work out an amicable settlement with you when he was so conveniently killed outside the club."

"And?" Damien stiffened.

The lawyer shrugged. "Everyone knows you and Tony didn't get along. In fact, I'm not sure whom you *did* get along with, besides your mother after her mind started to go. And that little scene at the cemetery was a nice touch. Too bad your manager got killed though."

Damien stilled. This was the second time someone had suggested – however obliquely – that he had offed his brother. First Dan, though only from the perspective of motive. And now the scumbag Maduro. And he didn't like it one bit.

He straightened and glared at Maduro. "If you have something to say, spit it out Esteban."

Maduro smiled with a pleasantness that contradicted his words. "I'm a reasonable man. I know you're in mourning. So is my client."

He grabbed the edges of his jacket and pulled them together over his paunch, then looked straight at Damien. "You've got two weeks to reach a settlement with Cristina. After that, on behalf of my client, I'll come after you with everything we've got."

"Get out." Damien turned on his heel.

"And Flores?"

"Yes?" Damien whirled about and glared at the lawyer.

"*Buenas noches* to you, too."

~ ~ ~

Mel had no intention of helping Damien when she'd intervened between him and Maduro. Frustrated by the unfairness of life, and particularly the unfairness of Damien's actions earlier in the day, what she really wanted to do was tell him off.

One look at Maduro's leering face had changed her mind. She'd be damned if she'd let Damien drag her on another hunting trip for evidence to use against her and her brother. She'd certainly never be fool enough to let him kiss her again. But for the moment he was still her boss, and she wasn't about to let some oily lawyer harass him at his own club. She could tell him off later.

But as it turned out, the night was busy and Damien was in an uncharacteristically bad mood, likely set off by Maduro's visit. Damien snapped at the waiters, yelled at Gord to bring more beer up from the back, and reamed out Becky for not keeping the popcorn machine full. When he disappeared into his office a half hour before closing, everyone heaved a sigh of relief.

The last tourists straggled out, the lights came up, and the staff did a quick clean and tidy of the club. Most had left by the time Mel glanced at the still-closed door to Damien's office. She was supposed to check in with him before leaving.

She knocked on the door and waited. There was no answer. She shoved the door open and stuck her head in.

Damien lounged back in his leather chair, his feet up on the desk beside a half-empty bottle of scotch. Stubble she hadn't noticed before shadowed his jaw, still bruised from Tony's funeral. From his bruised chin to black eyes and scowling face, he looked annoyed and dangerous. In his lap, he cradled a glass filled with the golden liquid, and a cigarette dangled from the corner of his unsmiling mouth.

She frowned.

"What?"

"You're drinking . . . and smoking?"

"Yeah, and I eat virgins for breakfast."

"What?"

He swung his feet to the floor and stubbed out the cigarette in an ashtray. It was the only stub. He looked at Mel, his expression flat. "I quit smoking eight years ago. I still like to have one every once in a while.

"And drink?" He raised his glass and swallowed the scotch in one gulp, then slammed the glass down on the desk. "You got something against drinking?"

"No. But –"

"Good." He grabbed a second glass from a shelf behind him, splashed in some scotch, and held it out to her. This wasn't quite the scenario she had played out in her mind during the long night shift.

She walked to the desk, and took the glass. The pungent aroma of the scotch hit her nostrils and she wrinkled her nose. She didn't like scotch. Actually, she rarely drank anything. Something to do with finding her mother and her latest lover in a drunken heap on the floor once too often, she assumed.

She swirled the scotch around in the glass, then looked at the bottle again. How many drinks had he had? She looked back at him. "I just came in to tell you I'm going home."

"And?"

She frowned. She was itching to give him a piece of her mind, but he was clearly spoiling for a fight. "And what?"

"Oh, come on." He snorted and sat back in his chair. His coal-black eyes drilled into her. "Don't tell me you didn't come in here to tell me off. Everyone else has."

She had, but she wasn't about to tell him that now. Instead she frowned. "Does this have something to do with Maduro?"

"Yes. No. Hell, drink your drink and go home. I'll call you a cab."

He reached for the phone but she put her hand on his to stop him. "What did Maduro say to you?"

For a moment she thought he was going to tell her to buzz off. His eyes burned with resentment and his scowl deepened. "Nothing that no one else hasn't said." With each word his tone grew more biting. "That I'm a heartless, greedy bastard. That I should sign the club and half of everything else over to Cristina."

Mel blinked. It was on the tip of her tongue to say now he knew what it felt like to be disrespected, but she resisted. Her fingers slid from Damien's hand, and she sat down in one of the chairs pulled up to the desk. She set down the drink. "Why would you do that?"

"Because it's the right thing to do. Because Tony should have had the club, not me. Because the charming, lovable younger brother had the club stolen out from under him by the no-good cop who, by the way, probably also had him murdered."

Mel was stunned. "Maduro said that?"

"Not exactly. More like an insinuation."

He swore. "Even my own lawyer thinks I should give the club to Cristina."

"You mean Salva? Alonzo Salva?"

"None other. He came by the house today after I dropped you off. Said he knew I was in an uproar over Tony and Ryan's death, but the sooner I did the right thing, the better it would be."

Mel frowned. "And why is giving Cristina the club the right thing?"

"Well, for a start, it would get everybody out of my face." He took another gulp of scotch, and looked at her hard. "You know, I never wanted any part of the family business. I only came back after *papa's* death because mama fired Tony and needed my help. It was never supposed to be permanent."

He sat up straighter and grimaced. "My job was supposed to be taking care of the club until Tony was better. But then a funny thing happened. The club started to grow on me. I can honestly say now I like it and would be sorry to give it up."

His dark eyes met hers, the pain and raw honesty she saw there touching her more than she liked.

"Giving it to Tony was one thing," he continued. "My brother lived and breathed that club. If not for the will, and my promise to my mother to take care of him, I'd have given it to him the day after mom's funeral. But Cristina?"

He gulped down the last of his scotch and sat back in his chair. He swore again, then continued, "Hell, I should just give it to her and get it over with."

Damien's torment only fueled Mel's dislike of Cristina. It didn't help that her own violent and fractured background made her suspicious of family ties at the best of times. She snorted. "Don't be a fool."

"What?"

"Seems to me your family has done nothing but suck you dry. But they're all dead now. Let 'em go. Cut 'em off – Cristina too – and get on with your life. It's what I'd do."

Damien stared at her as if he'd never seen her before. Skepticism radiated from him in waves. "Pretty strong words for a woman who gets upset when a brother she barely knows is a murder suspect. Are you trying to tell me that *you'd* cut Kevin off?"

"I already have," she said flatly. It wasn't exactly true, but she'd made no effort to contact him after he missed Darla's funeral, and had warned Joanie to not even think of taking him back. Cutting off her worry and concern for him was another matter.

"Hmph." His eyes narrowed. "So I guess you think I'm soft?"

"Could be." It was hard not to smile.

His scowl grew deeper, but there was a gleam in his black eyes that suggested he wasn't as angry as he looked. "You're sure this isn't just payback? Getting back at me for making you miss your interview this afternoon?"

"Nah. If this was payback, you'd be on the floor already."

"You think?" One eyebrow rose in a gesture that was part challenge, part cynicism.

Her stomach tightened but she didn't back down. "I know."

"Well then." He shoved aside the glass, stood up and sauntered around the desk until all six-foot-two inches of him loomed over her.

He held out his hand. "Let's say we put it to the test."

~ ~ ~

Assuming the fighting stance, one foot forward and her fists raised, Mel waited for Damien to make his first move. She wasn't quite sure how her decision to lecture him on what he should do had ended up here, barefoot on a mat under the lights on the dance floor in the empty club.

She'd thought he was kidding when he challenged her to a sparring match. Damien had stashed a couple mats from his wrestling days on the Key West Conch Wrestling Team in

Susan Haskell

one of the supposed bordello rooms upstairs and finally here was a perfect chance to put them to use. It turned out he also had a black belt in Taekwondo, and was even more desperate to work off the day's frustrations than she was. And who better than the bouncer who had boldly pronounced what he should do? *At least there were no witnesses.*

Now as they faced each other, poised to pounce, she couldn't say she was sorry. Not when Damien's dark eyes gleamed with challenge, and he stood lean and taut and dangerous and as sexy as hell in front of her. She felt it too, the rush of adrenalin that heightened her senses, the excitement building in her veins, the desire to provoke and best a worthy opponent. And another urge that had more to do with the memory of the brief kiss that simmered between them and the fact she was a woman and he was an attractive, powerful man. *Very* attractive.

"Sure you want to do this?" she taunted. "I don't want to hurt you."

"Pretty sure of yourself, aren't you?"

"Of course."

He nodded curtly and started to circle. Across from him, she did the same, watching him carefully, looking for weaknesses and trying to gauge the best way to attack. He had the obvious advantage of being stronger and bigger than she, but it was his skill, speed and smarts that were the issue. She knew her strengths – what she didn't know was her opponent's.

When it came, the sidekick was fast and without warning. At the last possible moment, she managed to block it from connecting with her head, then moved in and planted a solid punch to his chest. She followed it with a kick of her own to his shoulder, then jumped out of reach of his swinging leg.

"Had enough?" She couldn't hide her delight at landing the first hits.

His smile tightened. "Hardly."

Over the next few minutes, they landed an equal number of hits, but neither managed to incapacitate the other. Mel was impressed by the speed and cunning of some of his moves, but she was better at blocking and avoiding attacks and taking advantage of moments when he was off-balance or recovering from an attack. By the time she'd realized they were almost evenly matched, they were both huffing and puffing from the exertion.

"For someone who says he trains regularly, you're not in very good shape," she goaded.

"Yeah?"

Her taunt had the desired effect. He lunged. She ducked, then spun her leg around to kick the back of his head.

What happened next, she wasn't quite sure. One second she was delivering the decisive kick, the next she was flipping through the air. Her arms and back hit the mat with a resounding slap that knocked the air from her lungs. Before she could catch her breath, Damien was on her, his chest flattening hers, the weight of his body holding her down while his hands gripped her wrists like steel bracelets.

For a moment she couldn't catch her breath. His grin of satisfaction turned to concern. He lifted his upper body from hers. "You okay?"

She nodded, then gasped. "Yeah. You just knocked the air out of me." She gasped again. "What was that, anyway?"

He smiled. "Something special just for you. I thought you'd see it coming."

She winced. "Well, I didn't." She wriggled a little, testing his hold on her, looking for a weakness to exploit when the right time came, when . . . with a start she recognized the source of the heat between her legs.

Damien was aroused and pushing against her pelvis. And like a fool, she was melting around him.

She glanced up at him. Dammit, he knew. He was grinning like a Cheshire cat, and enjoying every minute of his power over her.

She sniffed. "If we were playing dirty, this is when I'd knee you in the balls."

He made a face. "Is that any way to treat your boss?"

He shifted his weight so he fit against her even more intimately, while still clamping her arms to the mat.

"You're no fun." She tried to ignore what they both knew was happening. "Okay. Let me up."

"Sure." But he didn't move. Instead, his lips turned slowly upwards in a charged smile that made the breath catch in her throat. "After I get my prize."

"What kind of pri . . . ?" Her mouth grew dry and her words trailed off as she saw the gleam in his dark eyes and knew exactly what it meant. What they'd been building to through the thrust and parry of their match, the sweaty encounters, the taunts. *Hell, what they'd been building to since they laid eyes on each other.*

His heated gaze focused on her lips, and slowly, inexorably, he dipped his head to hers to claim what they both wanted.

"This prize," he murmured. Then his mouth captured hers with a burning intensity that fanned every spark in her body. Gone was the tenderness, the sweet exploration of the first kiss. This kiss was hungry, fierce, taking what he wanted with the sureness of the victor.

It excited her no end. As her lips soaked up the delicious tastes and texture of his kisses, she strained for more. She was a prisoner, not of the lean male body pressing her to the mat, but of the need burning inside her too. A need inflamed by their conflict and the flirtation with danger.

She welcomed his kisses, with an urgency and passion she'd never felt before. When he increased the pressure and nudged her lips apart to deepen the kiss, she struggled against his hands holding her wrists. She wanted, needed, to touch him, to get closer still.

Finally he withdrew, nipping at her lips, nuzzling her throat, and rubbing his scratchy beard against her cheek. He pulled back a few inches to look at her, then glanced at the wrists he still held to the mat. He smiled. "You don't like to be held down, do you?"

"No. But not for the reasons you think."

He raised one eyebrow. "You trying to tell me you wouldn't have tossed me over your shoulder the moment I let you go?"

"I wanted to play too, is all."

"Really?" He smiled. Slowly his fingers slid from her wrists, and blazed a trail along the tender insides of her exposed arms. "Well, now I'm all yo–"

His hands hadn't reached her shoulders when she made her move. She rolled her back and knees forward at the same instant she shoved his shoulders up and away from her. He flipped over onto his back with a resounding crash.

He moaned and rolled over, then sat up and shook his head.

He smiled ruefully. "Well, I guess I should have seen that one coming." He rose to his knees and stood up. "So what are we calling this, a draw?"

She stood up and brushed off her clothes, then glanced at him scornfully. "A draw? Seems to me I won."

"Then what do you call this?"

He pulled her into his arms and captured her mouth in a kiss as hard, and fast and demanding as the swiftest reversal on the mat. Her knees grew weak and she felt dizzy and ravenous for his mouth on her and hers on him all at the same time. It didn't even occur to her to push him away. Desperately she pulled him closer, her hands twining in his thick hair, her breath fast and uneven under the assault of his kiss.

Finally, gasping, she pulled back. She caught her breath and smiled. "All right. It's a draw."

His smile widened, and he turned to retrieve his shoes and socks.

She smiled as she watched his trousers mold to his tight butt. *This time, maybe. We'll see about the next.*

~ ~ ~

Elation buoyed Damien up as he drove Mel home. But even as he was busy planning new and more intimate encounters, he began to realize that she was just as busy shutting down and shutting him out. By the time he pulled up at the curb on the quiet Meadow's street outside her house, there was little doubt.

Her expression sober, she turned to him. "You know this can't go anywhere."

His fingers tightened on the steering wheel. "Why not?"

"You know why."

He shook his head. "Oh, yeah. All those great reasons. I'm you're boss, you're my employee. Tony's death, Ryan's. The fact that your brother might be the killer."

He turned to her, willing her to look at him. "I don't see why any of that should affect this." Even as he said it, he knew he was wrong, but he forged on anyway. " What I do know is that I've had more fun tonight, with you, than I've had in months. You're not going to deny that you have too, are you?"

Her jade green eyes misted, taking the edge off their usual gem-like hardness. "No, but . . ."

He reached for her and kissed her with a tenderness that surprised even him. She responded in equal measure, then grasped the front of his shirt to pull him in closer.

He backed off, his forehead resting against hers. "Or that you don't want more of me?"

She swallowed. "I'm not denying it. I –"

"Mellie!"

A childish voice interrupted their conversation. Mel jerked away and looked out the window.

A bulging figure dressed in a flowing housecoat waddled barefoot towards them, a bundle in her arms. It took a while before Damien recognized her for the pregnant girl who had been at Ryan's funeral with Mel. Joanie, if he recalled. The girl who looked far too young to be pregnant, much less holding another child in her arms.

Mel was out of the car in a flash. "What are you doing out here?"

Joanie mumbled something Damien couldn't hear. Mel took the child from her arms and grasped it to her, then nodded towards the house. Obediently, Joanie headed back.

The baby in her arms, Mel glanced back at Damien. "Thanks for the ride." Without another word, she followed Joanie to the cottage.

Damien stared after her. Was the baby Joanie's?
Or was it Mel's?

Chapter Nine

Since Mel had plugged in the phone around noon, there had been no more of the heavy-breather calls that had sent Joanie running into the street with Kirsten in the early hours of the morning.

But Mel wasn't taking any chances. "Unplug the phone when you go to bed," she warned before she left for work. "And make sure all the doors and windows are locked."

"But what if the guy calls back before that?" Joanie sounded small and scared. She had been thoroughly rattled by the three nuisance calls that had woken her and Kirsten last night.

"Unplug the phone right away. And we'll get our number changed tomorrow. Okay? I don't like this any better than you do."

"Okay."

She didn't sound okay. Mel grimaced. Some days she felt more like Joanie's mother than her roommate. "Do you want to call one of your friends to come and stay with you? She could sleep on the sofa."

Joanie's eyes lit up, then just as quickly deadened again. She shook her head. "No, I guess not."

"Well, if you're sure." Mel scooped Kirsten out of the playpen and swung her through the air. Kirsten crowed with delight. "I'm going to work now, baby. You be good for Joanie, you hear?"

As she kissed the top of Kirsten's head, she had a fleeting vision of the shocked look on Damien's face this morning when he saw her take Kirsten from Joanie.

She'd been too worried to pay much attention, but now the meaning of that look hit her hard: *Damien thought she was Kirsten's mother.*

Which, for all intents and purposes, she was, but not in the way Damien thought.

Susan Haskell

Frowning, she set Kirsten down and picked up her purse from the table. Damien seeing her with Kirsten was probably the best thing that could have happened. As if there weren't already enough good reasons to ignore the crazy attraction that had flared between them, this one took the cake.

The big, bad bouncer with a black eye not only had a possibly murder-crazed brother, she had a baby, too.

She rolled her eyes. *Was she relationship material, or what?*

~ ~ ~

The moment Damien saw Mel walk through the door of the club, he wanted to pounce on her and demand the truth: Was that baby hers?

But he had to content himself with watching her breeze across the floor as she entered the bar. When he finally returned his attention to the man sitting beside him in the back of the room, he frowned.

"What?" He didn't like the bemused expression on Dan's face. Not one bit.

Dan nodded in the direction Mel had disappeared. "Sure you should be playing in that candy store?"

Damien reddened. He didn't need Dan to remind him. He already knew all the reasons he should stay away from Mel, but that didn't change the attraction he couldn't seem to resist, didn't want to resist. And oddly enough the baby - *if* it was her baby – didn't change his feelings in the least. It only intrigued him more.

He downed half his soda in one gulp. When he set it down, he ignored Dan's question and proceeded with his own. "Speaking of the bouncer, didn't you say you had news about her brother?"

Dan shook his head and sighed. "Based on the information you picked up yesterday at Shooters N Scooters, we got a warrant to search Kevin Saunders' place. He's sharing a trailer on Stock Island." He made a face. "If he's making any money on drugs, you wouldn't know it from his place."

"Find anything?"

"Some drug paraphernalia, a few bags with traces of crack and weed. But no weapons, no money, and no Kevin. Landlord says he's given notice for the end of the month. No one at the trailer park has seen him for days, and no one recalls seeing him with a scooter. Too bad you didn't collar him at the funeral yesterday. We could have brought him in for questioning."

Damien winced. Could have, should have, would have, none of it meant squat. "Anything else?"

Dan took his time, savoring the soft drink as if it were his favorite Key West Sunset Ale from World of Beer. It was half gone when he set it down and looked at Damien. "Got the skinny on the bullets. They were all fired from the same gun."

"Tony *and* Ryan?"

He nodded. "Yeah. A Colt .45."

Damien thought out loud. "This lends more credence to Cristina's suggestion that Ryan supplied Tony with coke the night of his death. And that Ryan had something to do with Tony's death."

Dan's expression didn't change. "Or at least knew who killed Tony."

Damien's fingers tightened around the cold glass. "It still doesn't sit right. Tony and Ryan were good friends. And Ryan was a huge help getting drugs out of the club after Tony was fired."

He paused. "Any drugs in Ryan? What did the medical examiner find?"

"Evidence of human growth hormone, but that's no surprise. You told me he was into bodybuilding. But no coke, no heroin, no needle marks, damage to his nostrils or lungs, nothing."

"You been following up on my brother's friends?"

"Yeah. But Cristina insists he dropped his friends from what she calls the 'bad old days' before he went into rehab. Apparently the only one who didn't get the message was Kevin Saunders. According to Cristina, he called Tony several times, until Tony finally told him to get lost."

Dan frowned. "Tony had pretty expensive digs for a guy who hadn't worked in eighteen months. How was he paying for everything?"

Damien sighed. "Mom paid for rehab. And when she died, she left the house to Tony and me. He needed cash, so I mortgaged it and gave him three hundred thousand."

"Hmm." Dan mulled that one over for a moment. "Was Cristina working?"

"She quit her job after Tony got out of rehab. Said she wanted to be around to support him. You know, see he was eating right, that he wasn't falling back into his old habits."

Dan leaned back. "Seems like Ryan's a big part of the missing pieces in this case. But some things about it don't make any sense."

He looked over at Damien. "Why would anyone kill Ryan at the cemetery, in front of all those potential witnesses, someone who might be able to identify the killer? Ryan lived alone and was out all hours of the night. There had to be plenty of other times when it would have been easier to get to him."

He swallowed the last of his soda. "Tony, too. There's no way his killer could have known that he was going to be outside Viva Zapata at that particular time."

Damien drummed his fingers on the bar. He had a pretty good idea where Dan was heading. "So?"

"So like I said after the knifing here the other night, maybe Tony wasn't the target. Maybe it wasn't Ryan or Cristina either." His eyes met Damien's. "Maybe it was you right from the start. You can't tell me that hasn't occurred to you."

Damien's jaw tightened. "But Saunders is supposed to be a crack shot. That's what the shooting guy in Marathon said. He shouldn't have missed, at least not at the cemetery. And as for the knifing, someone else would have had to be involved."

"His sister maybe?"

Damien shook his head. "I watched her like a hawk all night. Besides, he would have needed someone else to shut off the lights."

"That's *if* it was Saunders." Dan's eyes narrowed and he stood up. "Know of anyone else who wants you dead?"

~ ~ ~

Dan had barely dropped his bombshell and left when Cristina came stomping through the doors, Alonzo Salva at her side. Hands on her hips, eyes blazing, she scanned the room. Damien knew she'd found what she was looking for when her expression hardened and she stalked towards him.

He braced himself for the assault. He and Cristina had never gotten along, particularly in the weeks after his mama's death when Tony had been trying to get around the will and reclaim Viva Zapata. Since his death, they'd managed an uneasy peace, but now it looked as if the truce was over.

Eyes flashing, Cristina stopped in front of him. Alonzo scrambled to catch up.

"Why is that woman still working here?" The hysteria in her voice rose with each word.

"What woman?" he asked.

"You know exactly who I mean!" she shrieked. "That – that bouncer! The one who killed Tony!"

Alonzo came up beside Cristina. He looked at Damien and raised his hands in a gesture that said, "What can I do?"

"Mel didn't kill Tony," Damien said quietly. "She bounced him for throwing boiling coffee in Becky's face."

"How can you say that? You know she or Ryan gave him the coke. And her brother's the one who pulled the trigger."

She was about to poke him in the chest when he grabbed her wrist.

"That's enough, Cristina," he said. "We don't have all the facts yet, and until we do, she's staying. Just like all the other staff are staying. I have a club to run."

He continued in the same soothing tone. "Why don't you go home? It must be hard for you to be here . . ."

Her face crumpled and tears began to stream down her cheeks. Before Damien could say more she threw herself at him and started sobbing into his shoulder. "That's why I had to come," she gulped out between sobs. "I'm so lonely. I miss Tony so much . . ." The rest dissolved into sobs and she wrapped her arms around him.

Awkwardly Damien patted her back. Alonzo shrugged. "I tried to tell her to stay home. But she insisted on coming here. Said she had to see you."

Damien looked down at the weeping woman in his arms. Sobs wracked her slight form. He glanced at Alonzo. "Come into my office, both of you. We'll have a quiet drink there and let things calm down."

Only a few patrons stopped to stare as Damien, supporting Cristina and trailed by Alonzo, made their way across the length of the club and into his office. After settling Cristina on the couch crammed against one wall, he sent for a glass of Pinot Grigio for her and drafts for himself and Alonzo. By the time the drinks arrived, Cristina had stopped crying and set to work repairing her ravaged makeup. Alonzo sat down beside her on the couch and took a long swig of the cold draft.

Cristina replaced her mirrored compact in her purse, and turned to Alonzo. "Would you mind leaving for a few minutes? I'd like to talk to Damien alone."

Alonzo nodded. Clutching his draft, he rose to his feet. "No problem. I noticed a friend at the bar. When you want me, that's where I'll be."

Damien accompanied him to the door. Alonzo motioned him to come outside. When they were both in the hallway, he shut the door. "Sorry about the scene."

Damien shrugged. "It's not your fault."

Alonzo placed his hand on Damien's shoulder and moved closer. "I don't like to keep harping on the subject," he said. "But Cristina is worried about money. The sooner you clear up this question of the club or a share in the business, the sooner she'll leave you be."

Damien frowned. "How can she need money? She and Tony got three hundred thousand dollars from mama's house just six weeks ago."

"Yeah, but Tony had a lot of debts. And Cristina hasn't worked for over a year. Most of that money went to pay debts."

Damien's frown deepened. "I can give her some money to tide her over until –"

Alonzo shook his head. "You know, it would be a lot easier if you just swallowed your pride and gave her Tony's share of the business."

Anger coiled in the pit of Damien's stomach. Why had his own lawyer bought into the idea that he was the villain in this whole affair? Grasping, greedy Damien, who had to have everything, who refused to do the right thing by his brother's widow.

"I'd like to find Tony's killer first," he said. "Once that's resolved, then I can deal with everything else."

Alonzo smiled placatingly. "I hear you, Damien." He raised his glass to the closed door. "But you know Cristina."

"Yeah, I know Cristina." Damien sighed and turned to the door.

Back in the office, Cristina held the wine glass in one hand and stared blankly into space. She looked up when he came in, smiled and patted the burgundy leather couch beside her. Reluctantly Damien sat down, leaving a couple of feet between them.

She set her glass down on the paper-strewn coffee table and slid across the space separating them until her hip and thigh rested against his. She leaned back and sighed. "It's good to be close to you, Damien. You remind me so much of Tony."

Damien suppressed a hoot of derision. Grief had to have muddled Cristina's mind if she was comparing him to Tony. Sure, they looked alike, but that was the end of the resemblance. Tony had always been the social one, the one in the limelight, artistic, creative, dedicated to having a good time. Damien preferred the background, happy to follow his own interests in relative privacy while Tony shone. But out of respect for her grief, he let her go on.

Cristina took his hand and started playing with his fingers. "You have such nice manly hands." She smiled up at him, a tremulous smile that made him uncomfortable. Was she going to start crying again?

Suddenly she leaned forward and kissed him full on the mouth. He gaped and she deepened the kiss.

He jerked away from her. "What are you doing?"

She tried to pull his face to hers again. Her blue eyes were glassy and bright red blotches colored her cheeks. He avoided her, grasped her shoulders and held her at arm's length.

"Stop it. We both know you don't like me. You've never liked me."

Her lips trembled and tears started to pool in her blue eyes. "That's not true. I didn't like the fact you got Tony's club, but I never hated you. I just wanted Tony to have the club. He loved it so much. And now he's gone."

Tears began to fall in earnest, and she lowered her head to her hands. "I'm just so lonely." The heart-rending cry was muffled by her hands. "I feel so guilty."

Guilty? He frowned. Why did *she* feel guilty? He was the one with the guilt. Guilt because he'd broken his promise to their *mama* to watch out for Tony. Guilt because he'd been late for their meeting and Tony got murdered. Guilt because Tony had died without getting his precious club back. But Cristina?

He put his hand on her shoulder. "There's no reason for you to feel guilty. You were a wonderful wife to Tony."

Despite his words, he couldn't help wondering if the tears and the self-recriminations were a ploy to win his sympathy and make him settle with her faster. The thought had barely crossed his mind when her tears turned to sobs.

"But I am guilty. I am." She looked up slowly, her face contorted with pain. "And I'm so ashamed. I had an affair while Tony was in rehab."

"What?" Damien was shocked. "Did Tony know?"

She shook her head. "I don't think so. It only lasted about ten days, then I broke it off."

Damien frowned. "Why are you telling me this now?"

She shut her eyes and moaned. "I just feel so bad. I felt so guilty I quit my job when he got home. I wanted to make it up to him. But now I'll never be able to because he's dead."

Damien wasn't sure what to make of her confession. "Who was it?"

She wiped her face with the back of her hand. "Who was what?"

"The person you had the affair with. Your lover."

She shook her head. "That's not important. I knew it was a mistake right away, and so did he."

"You don't think this guy might have killed Tony?"

"No. It wasn't like that, Damien. It was just . . . an *aventura amorosa*. A stupid, dumb fling.

He let it go for now. In a day or two he'd get Dan to press her for the name. Just in case.

She sniffed and looked up at him with pleading eyes. "D'you think Tony would have forgiven me, Damien? Do you?"

"I know he would have," he said after a long moment of silence.

It was the kind answer. It was the merciful answer. But was it the right answer? He didn't know.

~ ~ ~

It was after four a.m. when Mel and Damien finally bundled the last tipsy customers off in taxis. Mel had found a young woman passed out in the washroom after last call, and it had taken some time to figure out who she was, where she was staying, and whether anyone would be there to take her in when the taxi dropped her off.

But now it was done. Mel stepped back from the curb and glanced at Damien. "Thanks for the help."

He nodded, but didn't turn from watching the taxi disappear up Duval.

A disappointment she couldn't quite quell filled her throat. The excitement and heat of last night had been a crazy aberration, and she knew it. Tony and Ryan's deaths loomed large between them, as well as Kevin's potential involvement, not to mention a lifetime of differences. And Kirsten, too. But despite her cynicism, despite everything she knew, through the long night a tiny part of her had kept alive the hope that maybe there could be something between them.

She straightened and headed back inside. *Twenty-five years old, the legal guardian of a little girl, and still an idiot!*

She had almost made it through the main room when there was a tug on her belt loop. The next thing she knew, Damien's arms were around her waist, her back against his lean chest. Warm lips whispered over her bare neck to her ear. His teeth tugged on her ear lobe. "So . . ." he growled, "you up for a rematch?"

She should have wrenched out of his arms immediately, but she let herself enjoy the warmth of his embrace just a little longer. "I don't think so," she said, wriggling her butt against his groin. "You really don't want to lose two nights in a row."

He laughed, then released her. "I thought it was a draw."

They walked companionably towards the bar. Only a few lights still shone on the deserted floor. "Everything's done now. I've got to –"

She didn't get to finish. Damien's mouth came down on hers at the same moment he swung her back against the wall. The banked fires of the night before exploded.

She didn't even try to hold back, just gave and took with everything she had. Her blood pounded, her heart raced as her temperature zoomed from zero to boiling point in five seconds flat.

Finally, panting, she withdrew to catch her breath. Her hands slid up to frame his face. "Wow. What was that?"

He grinned unabashedly and she'd never seen anything so beautiful. "Part of my nefarious plan to get you to come home with me."

Her heart leapt at the same time as good sense slammed on the brakes. "Uh-uh," as she slowly shook her head from side to side.

"Why not?"

"Reasons too numerous to mention. You know what they are." Her temperature cooled as they crashed across her mind.

He rested his hot forehead against hers. His eyes gleamed with that wolf-in-lamb's-clothing brightness. "Not even if I told you I needed a bodyguard?"

"A bodyguard?" She hooted. But the truth was she was having trouble thinking about anything but the lips only inches from hers and the hard evidence of his desire pressed against her pelvis.

She cleared her throat. "You with a bodyguard? I don't think so."

"I'm serious." The big hands pinning her to the wall started to massage her shoulders, the thumbs moving in erotic circles across her upper chest. "Even you thought that knife was meant for me the other night. And now Dan is suggesting that both Tony and Ryan were killed by mistake. That the real target was me. *Is* me."

An arrow of fear shot up Mel's spine. "You're kidding, right?"

"No."

She dropped her hands from his face and slid out of his embrace. "But you and your friend still think my brother is the main suspect? That he's trying to kill you?"

Damien grimaced. "'Fraid so."

She put her hands on her hips. "And you want *me* to go home with *you*?" She rolled her eyes. "You must really be desperate."

His dark eyes glittered with self-mockery. "Maybe. But only desperate for you." He paused and his gaze locked with her. "Just like you're desperate for me."

She didn't deny it, but when he raised a hand to touch her face, she moved out of reach and started for the bar. "Let's finish locking up. I've got to go home."

"Home to that baby of yours?"

She froze. She'd expected this, but after the last few heated minutes had thought he would let it pass. "Right," she said without turning to face him.

"Get a move on, then. I'll drive you home."

The silence continued through the last few minutes of closing, the walk to the car, and the first few blocks of the way home.

Mel watched Damien's hands on the steering wheel, strong, tanned, matter-of-fact. The same hands that had moved so erotically over her shoulders just moments before.

Her throat went dry. The hands she desperately wanted on her breasts, on her bare belly, *everywhere!* The hands she'd be a fool to let anywhere near her again.

"I checked your personnel records today."

She glanced over at him, but he was looking straight ahead at the road.

"You've worked without a break for the past two years. I don't imagine Russian Delights would be big on pregnant bouncers."

He turned to look at her. "So what's the story with the baby?"

"You don't need to know this."

"Maybe not. Tell me and I'll judge for myself."

Mel blew air out between her teeth. Why not? He already knew far too much of her family's dirty laundry.

"All right then," she said slowly. "Kirsten is ten months old. She's my niece. I got legal custody of her after my sister Darla died."

"Why not the father?"

She sniffed. "If I knew who he was. Even if I did, he's probably some loser."

"What's with the pregnant roommate who looks like she's twelve?"

"Joanie?" Mel smiled at Damien's description, exaggerated as it was. "She's twenty. I needed a dependable babysitter. She needed a decent home."

"What were they doing outside at four a.m. yesterday?"

Mel frowned. "Joanie was upset. Some jerk kept phoning and doing the heavy-breathing thing. She just needed reassurance when I got home."

Damien pulled onto her street. "Is that the first time?"

She shook her head. "No. We got the same calls the morning of Ryan's funeral. When I get up today I'll phone for an unlisted number."

Damien eased the car over to the curb in front of her house and put it in park. He turned and looked at her and shook his head.

"What?"

"You're one hell of a fraud, you know."

"*What?*" She pressed her lips together. If he was insinuating she –

"All this time I thought you were some tough, bad-ass bouncer from the wrong side of town, and now I find out you're a social worker."

"A social worker?"

A smile spread across his face. His eyes twinkled with more than a little humor as he rhymed off his reasons. "Adopting orphans. Taking in pregnant girls. Sticking up for ex-con brothers. Yep, a social worker."

Mel was speechless. She didn't understand him, or his reaction to her, at all. Physical attraction, fine. She felt it too. But she'd also been certain he was slumming, excited by the lure of the forbidden.

So what was this? Was he saying that he *liked* her, that he *admired* her?

Perplexed, she reached for the door handle and let herself out.

She blinked when she saw him get out the driver's side and slam the door. "What are you doing?"

The smile that he flashed at her across the top of the car took her breath away. "Coming in to see the baby."

"What? I –"

The roar of an engine drowned her out. She jerked around.

Susan Haskell

A two-stroke scooter burst down on them from White Street, its helmeted driver all in black. Over the ear-numbing drone came two shots in quick succession.

Mel dove for the ground. Out of the corner of her eye, she saw Damien grimace and clap one hand over his upper arm before he ducked down.

Chapter Ten

As the roar of the two-stroke receded, Mel inched up the side of the car. It was just in time to see the dark rider hunched over his black scooter boot it around the corner. It was too dark and too far away to see any of the license plate number.

She ran around the car. Damien lay on his side, holding his upper left arm.

"You've been hit!" She knelt down and tried to lift his hand away from the wound.

"Never mind me. Did you get the license?"

"No." She pulled out her cell. "I'll call 911."

"Take mine." He nodded to his right pant pocket.

She found his phone and tapped in the number. As it started to ring he sat up, took it from her and plastered it to his ear.

"It's Damien Flores, formerly of homicide. There's been a shooting on the 1300 block of Petronia. The shooter's on a black Zuma, with black helmet, armed and heading towards Eisenhower."

He grunted out a few more details, including the fact he'd been shot in the arm, then handed it back to her.

"The station's just around the corner. Police should be here in a minute or so." His eyes narrowed. "You're sure you didn't catch the license number? Not even part of it?"

"No."

Despite his admiring words a few minutes earlier, his manner suggested nothing had changed. He didn't trust her, not even to tell him the truth about the license plate of a guy who'd just tried to kill him. Red-hot attraction and sweet words didn't mean a thing.

"I couldn't tell what color of bike it was either," she said, her voice flat. "Just dark and noisy."

He didn't react. She hid her growing hurt with activity. "Let me see your arm."

When he didn't move she pushed his hand away. Blood streamed from a gaping, ragged hole on the outside of his upper arm. It was ugly, but didn't look too deep.

Without a word to him, she yanked his blood-spattered white t-shirt out of his pants. She took the hem and ripped, until she had a rough square of cloth that used to be the front of his shirt. She folded it and pressed it against his arm.

"Ouch!"

"What? The man's too big for my help, but can't take a little pain?"

"It's just a graze," he growled. "It can wait until the paramedics get here."

She lifted the folded cloth from his arm and frowned. "Looks pretty messy for just a graze." She pressed it firmly back in place, ignoring his wince.

Suddenly her stomach heaved and she felt cold and clammy. Damien could have been killed right here, in front of her home. She swallowed hard to keep back the nausea. This shooting was the kind of thing she'd tried to leave behind by moving here with Kirsten and Joanie.

But it wasn't working. Nothing was working. First Tony, then Ryan, and now Damien, though he was only wounded. Instead of getting away from the violence she hated, it was dogging her everywhere she went. Life wasn't getting better; it was getting worse.

The wail of sirens grew closer until it was ear shattering. Two police cruisers and an unmarked car squealed around the corner in a frenzy of light and noise. Two uniformed officers leapt from the first car, their Glock 17s drawn and ran towards them. The familiar figure of Dan Matthews stepped out of the unmarked cruiser and made his way more slowly to the curb.

Mel moved aside as the cops and Matthews approached Damien. Damien took over holding the cloth and continued pressing it to his arm. He knelt up and in a quiet, controlled voice described the events of the last few minutes.

Someone grabbed her arm. It was Joanie. Her eyes were big, her hair wild, and the terry housecoat that didn't quite close over her pregnant belly trailed several long threads. *Chicken*, freshly washed so extra silky, hung out of her pocket. "What happened?"

Mel nodded towards the Infiniti parked at the curb. "Someone shot at Damien when he got out of the car." Out of nowhere, fear gripped her. "Kirsten. Is she all right?"

"She's sleeping. The sirens woke me up, so I came out to see what was going on."

Mel studied Joanie. She looked far calmer than she had the night before. "What about the mouth breather? Did you get any calls?"

"Only one, around midnight. I unplugged the phone, and it's been fine."

"Good. I'll arrange for an unlisted number as soon as I get up. But why didn't you unplug the phone sooner?"

Joanie hung her head and fingered the toy chicken. "I was kind of hoping Kevin would call."

"Oh, Joanie!" Mel sighed. When would her roommate accept the truth? *Chicken* or no *Chicken*, Kevin wasn't coming back. And with all the police suspicion of him, it was better if he didn't come around here anyway.

Suddenly she was overwhelmed with fatigue. "Why don't you go back in and check on Kirsten? I'll be there in a minute."

Joanie nodded and trundled off. Mel watched her round the corner of the house, then she walked to the sidewalk and down the street a few feet. The earsplitting noise and light had awakened the neighbors, who stood in nightclothes on their front lawns or silhouetted in doorways. Some of them were talking and waving their hands, upset and agitated that their quiet little street had been attacked by violence.

And well they should be. Mel didn't like it either. When she'd moved to this little cottage, it had felt as safe as a church sanctuary.

But now? Nuisance phone calls, shootings? What could possibly be next?

The fact that Damien had been shot only made it worse. It was starting to look as if his bald-headed friend was right; Damien, not Tony or Ryan, was the killer's real target.

In the cool night air, Mel shuddered. She rubbed her arms but the friction wasn't enough to rid her of the bone-deep chill that permeated her entire body.

She stared in the direction the black-robed shooter had disappeared. Everything about him, from his sudden appearance out of nowhere to the blaze of the pistol from his black-gloved hand made her uneasy, in ways she couldn't even begin to explain.

Was it Kevin? She shut her eyes. God, she hoped not.

~ ~ ~

Despite a poor sleep, Mel took care of changing their phone number as soon as she got up. An unlisted number was going to cost more money she didn't have, but at least the phone company didn't need to come on site to make the change. She needed to keep a landline as long as Joanie was looking after Kirsten.

The afternoon sun streamed into the living room through the sliding doors opening into the backyard. Mel sat at the diminutive kitchen table, drinking her third coffee of the day, and watching Kirsten play on the floor with a set of brightly colored plastic blocks. Or perhaps she should say watching Kirsten try to *eat* the blocks. One by one, the child picked up a red or green or blue block, and raised it to her mouth. Each time she chewed on a corner, then sat back, a look of puzzlement on her chubby face. Then she discarded the block for another, and the process repeated itself.

Mel watched the little girl with envy. Had there ever been a time in her life when she'd been so innocent, so intent on understanding and exploring her own tiny world? Probably, but she didn't remember it. Her job now was to see that Kirsten stayed in that sweet, safe world as long as possible.

The thought reminded her of Damien's last words to her before he'd been shot in the early hours of the morning. He'd called her a social worker. *Ha. As if.*

That compliment had only made his suspicion of her a few minutes later all the more bitter.

But it was just as well. If she needed another warning that she'd been a fool to engage in any kind of relationship with Damien beyond employer/employee, there it was. Because no matter what he said, no matter who was charged with these murders, she would always be the suspicious bouncer, with the even *more* suspicious brother.

It was unfair, but she was used to that. Winning the right to be Kirsten's legal guardian hadn't been easy. Everything from her lifestyle and income to her parenting skills had been questioned. If it hadn't been for the testimony of her former foster parents Don and Betty Leeson, she might never have gotten the chance.

She glanced down at Kirsten again. Damien's suspicion had reminded her all too sharply of her tenuous hold on Kirsten, and how easy it would be to lose her. No way that was going to happen. Even if she had to find Kevin herself and prove his innocence once and for all. As long as *she* knew the truth, it wouldn't matter what anyone else thought.

She stood up, surprised it hadn't occurred to her to look for Kevin before. She scooped Kirsten up from the floor and swung her around. "Hey, baby. Gonna go-a-hunting with me?"

The doorbell rang. Mel settled Kirsten on her hip and walked across the living room. She opened the door to a middle-aged woman with tight, greying curls. She was conservatively dressed, in a thin plaid jacket, navy skirt and plain, low-heeled pumps, and carried a brown leather briefcase. From the practiced neutral expression on her round face to the choice of clothes and folio, everything about her screamed 'social worker'. *And not the kind Damien had been talking about, either.*

The woman's gaze fell on Kirsten, and then rose to Mel's face, settling on the yellow bruises that were all that remained of her black eye from a week ago. She frowned. "Miss Saunders? Melissa Saunders?"

Involuntarily Mel clutched Kirsten more tightly. "Yes?"

Susan Haskell

The woman did not smile. "I'm Leticia Raymond. I'm an investigator from the Department of Children and Families. I need to talk to you."

Mel's first reaction was to slam the door in the woman's face, but she fought it off. "And why?" she summoned her sweetest possible voice.

"The child abuse hotline has received a serious complaint about your care of your niece."

~ ~ ~

His bouncer was on the warpath, and Damien didn't know why. At first he'd thought Mel was just having a run of Viva Zapata's more troublesome customers, but as the night wore on, he saw a pattern. She wasn't resolving problems as she usually did. She was provoking them. It was almost as if she were looking for any opportunity to lash out.

As she made her rounds, she shoved aside any customer who got in her way. She collared and ejected a couple of happy drunks where a warning should have sufficed. She roughed up at least one guy who had the temerity to make an obscene remark, and she glared at anyone who dared look at her with anything even mildly resembling a leer.

But when she planted her boot on the backside of a frequent local and literally kicked him out the door, Damien had seen enough.

He grabbed her arm as she came through the doors. "We need to talk."

The look that shot from her hard green eyes was lethal and put every sense in his body on alert; for a moment he thought she was going to haul off and slug him. But all she did was yank her arm free. "All right."

Once inside the office, he whirled around. "What the hell's gotten into you?"

"Nothing." Her face set in stubborn lines.

"You call picking fights, shoving customers around, and kicking our regulars out the door nothing? There's something wrong. I want to know what it is."

Not an eyelid flickered, not a muscle twitched in her mulish face. Her full lips stayed in the same unforgiving pout that always annoyed and turned him on at the same time.

He sighed in frustration. The ache from the wound in his left arm throbbed worse than it had only minutes before. "This isn't some weird reaction to the fact I was shot last night, is it? Your twisted way of showing how much you care?"

His sarcastic comment didn't elicit as much as a hint of humor. "No," was her short obstinate reply.

"What is it then?" He was torn between shaking her or throwing her to the ground for that sexual encounter they'd both been flirting with far too long.

Something in his expression must have warned her. Her eyes flickered once, and she stepped back. "Look, I promise to be good for the rest of the night. You don't need to know more than that."

"Actually, I do."

The scowl returned. "Why?"

He met her angry gaze with a challenge of his own. "Because I want to know everything about the woman I'll be making love to later tonight."

Chapter Eleven

"What are you talking about?" Mel demanded, pent-up anger and frustration sharpening her words.

Damien's voice lowered to a seductive growl. "Exactly what I said. After my brush with death last night, I decided there's no time to waste. I want to make love with you. Here. Tonight."

Without warning, tears welled in her eyes. She muttered the first obscenity that came to mind. "Are you sure a bullet didn't take out your brains? I saw the way you looked at me after you were shot. You think I lied to you about not seeing the license plate."

"What?" Surprise flickered across his face. "Why would you think that?"

"Because you don't believe anything I say." Exasperation made her voice rise. "No matter what crap you say about admiring me, whenever something happens, you suspect me first."

"Mel . . . Mel . . . Mel . . ." He looked as exasperated as she felt. He gestured to the chair. "Sit down for a few minutes. There's something I need to tell you."

Her first compulsion was to bolt, but she forced herself to follow him to the sofa. She sat down as far away from him as she could manage.

His dark brown eyes were warm and serious. "I was a police officer for almost ten years, a detective for the last five. I'm used to regarding witnesses with skepticism – all witnesses, no matter who they are, no matter what they have to say. Old habits die hard. Just because I looked skeptical, doesn't mean I don't believe you." He paused. "Really."

She exhaled sharply, wavering between accepting and refusing his explanation. Everything in her experience told her that trusting him was a one-way street to pain and humiliation. For *her*, not him. But she was also honest enough to know that a large part of her anger was misplaced, the product of today's visit from the social worker.

"All right." She started to get up. "I'd better go –"

"Not so fast." He pulled her over to the sofa, and this time she landed right beside him. "We're not finished yet."

Her eyes widened. "You're not crazy enough to think that –"

"No. Not yet." He grinned. "I want you to think about *that* for the rest of the evening, until you're as hot for me as I am for you."

"You *are* crazy!"

"Maybe. Crazy for you." His grin faded. "But that's not what I meant. You still haven't told me why you're so upset. My ego's big, but not so big that I think you'd be that upset just because I didn't believe you."

Her first inclination was to push him away. "I'm fine."

She started to rise again and he pulled her back down. "No, you're not." This time he hung onto her hand, and his tantalizing warmth seeped into her.

"It has nothing to do with you."

"No?" He lifted one eyebrow. "When you start bashing my customers for no reason, I'd say it has plenty to do with me."

She winced. He was right, but . . .

"Maybe I can help."

"And maybe you can't." She pulled her hand from his. She took a deep breath and looked away, certain that what she was about to tell him would only make him more suspicious. "I had a visitor from Department of Children and Families today."

"Yeah?"

She steeled herself to say the words. "It was an investigator. She was looking into an anonymous complaint to the child abuse hotline. The caller said I . . . I hit Kirsten. He said I brought different men to my cottage every night. He said I left Kirsten alone, screaming in her crib, for hours every day."

In the silence that followed, Mel didn't dare look at Damien for fear she would lose it. Instead, she stumbled on. "The social worker examined Kirsten, talked to me, and then Joanie when she got home. She also went to the main cottage and talked to Mr. and Mrs. Rubenstein, and then she called my doctor."

When Damien finally spoke, his voice was gentle and deep. "You still have Kirsten, don't you?"

"For now. The social worker seemed satisfied it was a crank call. But the complaint and the investigation will be a matter of record. If anything else happens, they'll review the complaint and wonder if it was true."

The cushions shifted. The comforting strength of Damien's arm settled around her shoulders. "I'm sorry. I know how much you want to keep your niece with you."

She looked at him then and knew he meant what he said. But she shook her head. "I don't think so. You can't possibly know what it's like to have someone you don't know try to destroy your life. To have things you can't control – your background, your family – rise up to drag you down again and again. To have people suspect you just because of who you are."

His face darkened but he let it pass. "Any idea who the caller might be?"

She shook her head. "A neighbor? A wacko? I don't know."

Damien tilted her face towards his. Slowly, gently, his mouth brushed hers, in a kiss so tender and comforting and unexpected that it took her breath away. It was all she could do not to cling to him.

He kissed her again, and they rose together from the sofa. "Go on out there now and behave yourself."

His lips brushed her forehead this time and he smiled, his dark eyes alight with promise. "I'll see *you* later."

~ ~ ~

Becky's empty tray clattered onto the bar. While she waited for Gord to prepare her umbrella drinks, she talked to Mel. "I'm glad your talk with Damien has calmed you down.

It was beginning to look like you were going to rip the place apart."

Mel winced as she leaned against the bar. She glanced at Becky. The smaller woman had recovered remarkably well from the coffee burns, probably because of Gord's quick action with the cold compresses. Her confidence and good nature had resumed as the blisters had healed, and her appearance had returned to almost normal. Despite her friendliness, Mel had been reluctant to confide in her, particularly about Kirsten. It was bad enough that she had confessed to Damien about the complaint to the child abuse hotline.

Becky continued her friendly chattering. "I'm thinking we should agitate for danger pay. After what happened to me, Tony and Ryan's deaths, that knifing, your black eye, and now Damien – who knows what's going to happen next?"

Mel shrugged. "Like Damien would go for *that*."

"Oh, I don't know." Becky turned from the bar. Mel followed her gaze to where Damien crossed the dance floor on his way to the grand staircase to the second floor. He stood tall and straight in his navy sports jacket, and his stride was strong and confident. The jacket hid the dressing and bandage on his left arm, and the casual observer would never know he'd been shot the night before.

Despite herself, Mel's pulse quickened and a flash of heat arrowed from her breasts to her belly. His words burned across her mind. *"Because I want to know everything about the woman I'll be making love to later tonight."*

"I mean if *you* asked him."

That brought her back hard to reality. "What?" Mel frowned. "If I asked him what?"

Becky's blue eyes sparkled. "Don't play innocent with me, Mel. I've seen the way he looks at you. And the way you look at him. Nor has it escaped my notice - or anyone else's – that you close up most nights together. And he *was* shot outside your house in the wee hours of the morning."

Mel stiffened. She knew Becky meant well, but she didn't like anyone knowing her business. Especially since whoever shot Damien seemed to know her business too.

A chill ran down her spine. Clearly the same thought had occurred to the police too. That detective friend of Damien's had been around earlier tonight. He'd interviewed every staff member, including her, and pressed her again and again about any problems with staff or clients that might have led to a vendetta against Damien. Already distracted by the visit from the social worker, his questions had only put her more on edge.

Tight-lipped, she responded to Becky's crack. "It doesn't mean anything."

"Of course not." Becky picked up the tray of drinks and heaved it to her shoulder. "Actually, I think it would do you both good."

"What would do us both good?"

Becky grinned and leaned over to whisper in Mel's ear. "Getting naked together, of course!"

~ ~ ~

Damien started turning off the lights as Mel came into the main room from the hallway after doing her regular check of the washrooms.

He paused in his work to watch her walk over to the bar. The earlier agitation and tension in her movement was gone, replaced by the long, sure strides he loved; her shoulders back, head up, as if she owned the room and everyone in it. He liked the way her black, sleeveless top and spandex flares clung to her figure, emphasizing her feminine curves without apology or artifice. His temperature rocketed as his mind conjured images of what lay beneath all that clinging black.

His fingers paused on the last of the switches for the overhead lights and fans dangling from the high ceiling. He knew exactly what he wanted, complications be damned. The question was, did she want it as much as he did?

"I'm finished." She turned to face him, her expression closed. "I can find my own way home."

He frowned. This was not part of his plans. "Yeah? Why?"

"It's just better that way."

"Better for who?" He flicked off the last of the lights, then started across the floor to the bar. The only illumination came from the clerestory windows high above.

"Both of us. You can go straight home to rest and start mending and I –"

He didn't give her a chance to finish. He crowded her against the bar, corralling her between his arms. "You can what? Spend money you need for Kirsten on a taxi home? I don't think so. Besides, I don't want rest."

The lower half of his body brushed hers, the bulge at his groin making it clear what he did want if his earlier words hadn't. The deepening color of her eyes, from sea green to dark jade, and the slight catch in her breath, indicated she knew too.

"Since I was shot last night, I've been doing a lot of thinking."

"About what?"

"About living in the moment. About not worrying over complications, what could have been, what might be." He paused to linger in the beauty of those green depths. "About how good we'd be together."

"You think?" Her pelvis moved slightly against his, belying the question in her eyes, the faint furrow across her brow.

"I know." He leaned into her, almost sighing aloud in satisfaction from the intimate contact. His gaze flickered to her lips, then back to her eyes. "Why not? There's no one here except us. We can do anything we want, anywhere we want."

Slowly her lips curved upwards. She raised her face to his and he lowered his head. Suddenly she jerked back in alarm. "What about your arm?"

He smiled. "What arm?"

"Is it okay? I don't want to hurt you."

"There's no way you're gonna hurt me." His smile widened. "Besides, I'm a man. I can take it."

Hungry for her taste, he sought her lips. His mouth came down on hers, and his arms slid around her back. She stepped into his embrace, the eagerness of her response fanning his desire. His hands started to slide under her top when she grabbed his wrists and pulled back.

"What?"

Her smile was cheeky. "I guess this means I can't throw you around for foreplay, right?"

He hooted with laughter. "I'm sure you'll think of something better."

He cupped her chin and captured her lips once more.

~ ~ ~

It was crazy. It was dumb. But Mel was past ready to shut out the world for a few minutes alone and naked with Damien. A few minutes when it didn't matter that her brother was a murder suspect. A few minutes when she could forget about the struggle to keep Kirsten and make a good life for them both.

What she wanted was to love Damien, and to be loved by him. She wanted his hands caressing her, his mouth and tongue tasting and lapping at every heated inch of her, his lean, naked body wrapped around her and satisfying the yearning that had been taunting her since she'd first met him. And she wanted it now, before all possibility was snatched away by time and events she couldn't control.

Seeing him gunned down in front of her cottage should have been a signal to run as fast and far away from him as possible. The death of his brother, the suspicions about her brother, her responsibility for Kirsten – all of them should have only made her run faster. But for reasons she didn't quite understand, her heart rebelled. She didn't want to run. She wanted Damien, and she wanted him now, even if it was only for a few brief moments in the middle of the night.

Eager and hungry, she stepped into his embrace, every part of her tingling in anticipation of their lovemaking. Damien's gunshot wound impeded him only a little. Her head swimming and her bones melting, she hardly noticed that she helped him out of his jacket and t-shirt, or that he couldn't quite manage to pull her tight top over her head.

Instead she lost herself in the electricity of his touch, alternately hard and demanding and exquisitely slow and gentle. His mouth worked magic on the tender skin of her throat, on her aching breasts, and the sensitive flesh of her belly and inner thighs. Everything he touched came alive, fueling her edginess and sharpening her need for him until she could think of nothing else.

Her lips skimmed the line of his jaw, reveling in the roughness of his five-o'clock shadow. She sipped from the taut skin over his collarbones. She trailed kisses across the flat of his chest to his lightly furred belly and beyond, and still it wasn't enough. When she finally lay naked beneath him, flat on her back on the smooth cool wood top of the bar, every part of her ached to have him inside her.

But not so much that she didn't notice his wince of pain when he hovered over her. Without a word, she slid out from under him, prodded him onto his back, and straddled him. Surprise, then delicious knowing flickered in his dark eyes, and her heart swelled to overflowing. She grinned down at him.

"You probably don't know that I once won the Sexy Bull Riding contest at Cowboy Bills."

He laughed at the news.

"Well, cowboy, . . . this ride's on me."

His response was to reach for her, pulling her down to him for more of those killer kisses that made her forget everything except the taste and texture of his mouth. She rocked against him, slowly rebuilding the tension that pulsed through their bodies, luxuriating in the feel of him inside her, wanting to give him as much pleasure as he was giving her. Her breath ragged, her heart pounding, she pulled back from his kisses. Hands propped on her thighs, she drove them both higher and higher, her gaze drinking in his flushed face and glazed eyes, as high on her power to give him pleasure as the overwhelming sensations swept through her own body.

Triumph and satisfaction flooded through her. Murmuring in contentment, she slowly lowered herself to his chest. His one good arm tightened around her, as she laid her head against his shoulder. In the silence of the room, she could hear his still racing heart.

The minutes passed. Their breathing slowed and became more regular. The cool night air and the yeasty smell of beer and spirits began to invade the warmth created by their lovemaking. Mel was reluctant to move or speak or do anything that would end the spell and shatter the moment of closeness.

Beneath her, Damien shifted slightly. Then one arm slid from her back and grappled beneath him for something. A moment later his shoulder moved, and a cool breeze wafted down on her. "What's this?" he asked.

She squinted upwards. Arm's length above her head, he waved around a tiny scrap of black material. Her thong.

"Give me that!" Her arm shot out to grab it, but he yanked it to the side and out of her reach. His left arm held her down with as much power as if he'd never been wounded.

Just out of reach he continued to twirl the tiny scrap of cloth. She knew without looking he was grinning.

"Why am I not surprised that this is black?" he asked. He tilted his head to look at her. "Do you own any clothes that aren't black?"

"Of course."

"Yeah? Like what?"

"I have jeans and –"

"Jeans?" He chuckled, a low, sexy rumble from deep in his throat that set her nerve endings tingling again. "That hardly counts. They're almost black."

She sniffed. "I've got a couple of white t-shirts. And a white bra. And . . ." Her voice trailed off as she realized he was right.

His lips brushed the top of her head and he gathered her close again. "Why all the black? Is there some secret reason or is it just that you know how incredibly sexy it makes you look?"

His words filled her with warmth. "Actually, it's cheaper and more practical to have all your clothes one color. But it's also part of my business strategy."

"Your business strategy?" Amusement colored his deep voice.

"Sure." She struggled back out of his arms and into a sitting position on the bar beside him. "Black makes me look dangerous. In my job, that's a bonus. No one wants to mess with the scary chick. Which is great, because I'm not looking for a fight. Or a relationship."

He propped himself up on his good arm and studied her for a moment. The humor had fled from his face. "The fight I understand, but the relationship?" He nodded at her and the bar on which they lay. "What exactly do you call this?"

She stilled, and an unaccustomed flush crept up her neck. "That's different."

He reached up and caressed her breast, his thumb drawing circles around her nipple until it blossomed under his touch. "How so?"

"It just is."

"Good." A smile stretched across his face, lighting his eyes and touching her heart in a way nothing had before.

"Because it's going to take a lot more than black underwear to scare me away."

~ ~ ~

When the Five 6's taxi pulled up in front of Mel's house, Damien moved to open the door. Mel touched his arm and shook her head. "It's you who were shot the other night, not me. Stay in the cab. I'll be fine."

He opened his mouth to protest and she cut him off with a kiss that went on for close to a minute. She didn't care what the taxi driver thought.

Finally, she pulled back and grinned. "Goodnight, Mr. Flores."

"I'm getting out –"

"No." She glared at him. "I'll be fine. Just fine. If you want, you can watch until I get safely into the back yard."

Damien glared back. "Anyone ever tell you how stubborn you are?" He sat back, suddenly quite exhausted. "Okay. But I'm waiting until I can see you're okay."

"Bossy, aren't you?" she teased as she reached for the door handle. She opened the door and looked back at him. "It's a good thing I like you."

She got out and shut the door. Despite the fact she'd normally be in bed asleep by now, there was a spring in her step that hadn't been there before. All her responsibilities, her fears, had receded into the background. She felt lighter than air, happier than she remembered being in years. Maybe this was love, maybe it wasn't. Whatever it was, it was wonderful.

She had to force herself to walk, not skip, across the lawn. When she reached the corner of the cottage, she turned and waved, then waited for the taxi to pull away.

As Damien disappeared down the street, she raised her palm and blew a kiss after him. It was a silly gesture, and totally unlike her, but she didn't care. Time enough tomorrow to figure out how making love to Damien had changed things, for better or for worse.

She turned down the walk to her cottage. As usual, the lamp over the door was on, casting a circle of welcome light over the stoop and the slightly overgrown hot pink bougainvillea that bordered it. "Maybe I'll take up gardening," she said out loud as she smiled to herself.

What wasn't usual was the heap of what looked like dark clothing dumped on the front doorstep.

The hair on the back of Mel's neck prickled. Something wasn't right.

She crept forward. As she got closer, the heap of clothing took form. An arm, a twisted leg, a hand, all of it covered in black cloth or leather, *and none of it moving.*

And pooled in the cracks in the cement walk, a dark, viscous liquid that could only be blood.

Chapter Twelve

Mel's stomach heaved; for a second she thought she was going to be sick. Willing her body to behave, she forced the nausea down, then crept forward.

She knelt beside the crumpled form. Whoever it was, wasn't moving. The body lay face down, a black cap covering the brown straggly hair that lay in strands on what looked like a man's neck. Everything he wore was black, from his shoes and socks and jeans, to the leather jacket, gloves and wool hat. *Just like the man who attacked Damien the other night.*

She pushed past a shiver of fear to press her fingers against his neck. The flesh was cold and still. As she raised her gaze from his neck, she saw something even more ominous: a semi-automatic pistol gleaming in the overhead light, lying a few feet away on the walk.

She jerked back from the body, pulled her cell from her pocket and tapped 911. When the dispatcher came on the line, she had to center herself once more and clear her throat before she could speak. "This is Melissa Saunders. A man's been shot outside my door. I think he's dead. There's a gun here too."

She rattled off her address and was about to hang up when the dispatcher suggested she look at the shot man again. Maybe she could do something for him while waiting for the police and ambulance.

She took the phone from her ear so she could roll the guy onto his back. She supported his neck and back as she gently rolled him over. She eased her hands out from under him, and put the phone back to her ear.

Her gaze flitted over the guy's blood-soaked chest and upwards to his bearded face. "I'm just going to – "

Her voice died and the cell phone fell from her suddenly lifeless fingers.

"What's going on? Has something happened? Are you still there? Ms. Saunders?"

The dispatcher's voice, tinny and far away, tinkled at the edge of her consciousness. Mel couldn't have answered even if she'd wanted to.

Because the bloody heap lying on her doorstep wasn't just some heartless killer.

It was her brother. It was Kevin.

~ ~ ~

The clump of heavy shoes on the path from the front cottage, loud voices, sirens, shouts, flashing lights – all had conspired to awaken Kirsten. And once awake, nothing Mel did could induce the agitated ten-month-old to go back to sleep. Whenever she tried to put her down, she immediately started to wail. And Joanie was no help. Ever since she'd learned of Kevin's death, she'd been curled up in her housecoat on the couch, alternately crying and clutching little *Chicken* to her chest.

Mel shifted Kirsten from her left to her right shoulder. Gently she bounced her and patted her on the back, while murmuring soothing sounds. Though the child was quiet for the moment, she felt stiff and tense, and her big, tear-filled eyes turned to follow each new person to enter the kitchen. It was as if she sensed Mel's agitation and was inviting her to join in a wail of pain and frustration.

But Mel had to stay calm, sane, in control, for no other reason than to be able to answer the incessant questions that Damien's friend, the Kojak clone, had been firing at her from the moment he'd arrived.

"So tell me again; when was the last time you saw your brother?"

Mel's temper flared. Surely she'd answered that question at least ten times before. "I told you already," she bit out. "I'm sure Damien told you before too. At Ryan's funeral. Kevin was in the hallway near the washrooms at the funeral home. He gave me a stuffed toy to give to Joanie."

"Have you still got the toy?"

Blood Ties in Key West

"Yes." Mel glanced at Joanie. The toy chicken was pressed to her face and she was weeping into it.

Matthews grimaced. "I'd like to have it tested."

"If you can get it away from her." Mel shifted Kirsten back to her shoulder. "What do you want it for anyway? She's already washed it. It's not going to tell you anything."

"We'll see." Matthews sighed. "Okay . . . Again . . . Any idea why your brother might have come here tonight?"

"I told you that Joanie is carrying his baby." She glanced over at her again. Joanie was oblivious to everything but her own misery. Matthews had given up trying to get anything coherent out of her.

The bald-headed detective's eyes narrowed. "Any reason you didn't reveal that little gem earlier?"

"Because it's none of your business," she snapped. "Besides, Kevin hasn't seen or talked to Joanie for months."

"At the funeral, did Kevin do anything or say anything besides give you the toy?"

"He said he was sorry about Ryan."

"Sorry?" Matthews's voice vibrated with heightened interest. "Why sorry?"

Mel looked at him with disbelief. "Sorry about his death, I assume. That's what people normally say at funerals."

"Why would Kevin care about Ryan's death?"

Mel shifted her weight back and forth. "We were neighbors in Bahama Village. Ryan and Kevin were friends up through middle school."

"And now?"

She shook her head. "Don't know. I'm assuming that Ryan hasn't seen Kevin since before he went to prison. If Ryan had, he didn't tell me."

"Besides the funeral, when did you last see your brother?"

"It was before he went to prison."

"What'd he go to jail for?"

"You know better than me."

"I'd like you to tell me."

"A drug charge of some kind. I don't remember."

"You don't remember?" Matthews's lip curled. "You expect me to believe that?"

Mel stiffened. She was fed up with people not believing her, of always assuming the worst. She bit back her irritation. "We weren't close. I haven't lived with any of my biological family since I was eleven. I saw Kevin only a few times when I was a teenager, and not at all after my sister died."

"What about the gun? The one lying beside your brother's body? You ever seen it before?"

She shook her head. She had a pounding headache, and her eyes were dry and stinging. She wished she could cry, like Joanie and Kirsten. But instead she had to hold it together and answer all these damn questions.

Matthews pushed on relentlessly. "We haven't tested it yet, but you realize it's a Colt .45."

"How would I know?"

"The same type of gun fired the bullets that killed Tony and Ryan, and wounded Damien. We know those bullets all came from the same gun. The only thing we don't know yet is whether this is *the* gun."

The implication was inescapable; Matthews thought her brother had killed Tony and Ryan, and tried to shoot Damien. Probably tried to knife him too.

Mel's stomach clenched and she pressed her lips together hard. *But did anyone care who had killed Kevin? Or did they all believe he'd killed himself?*

A high-pitched wail right beside her ear was a precursor of a new, full-fledged screaming fit from Kirsten. Mel shifted the child about, bouncing her gently and cooing to her, but it was no good.

Matthews persisted over the baby's screams. "Can you think of any reason why your brother would kill Tony Flores? Or Ryan Ronson? Or Damien?"

Kill Damien. The words stabbed painfully through her gut and brought back haunting images. Gunshots in the night. Damien down on the ground and bleeding. A dark-clothed figure fleeing into the night on his scooter. Damien's black eyes gleaming with heat and excitement as she hovered naked over him on the bar . . .

Her grip tightened on the thrashing baby. She fought back the urge to join her crying. NO, Mel wanted to scream. NO, her brother wouldn't do it. He wouldn't try to kill Damien, hadn't killed Tony and Ryan. But the truth was, she hardly knew her brother. Maybe she'd never really known him. How could she *possibly* know what he was capable of or what he'd done?

Instead, she pressed her lips together and shook her head.

"What's his address?"

"I don't know." Her voice was hoarse even to her own ears. Clearly Matthews was trying to trip her up by asking her questions to which he already knew the answers. He was taking advantage of the shock of her brother's death, the fatigue, the shrieking baby, trying to get her to admit to *something . . . anything.*

Did he actually think that she was involved or had known something about the shootings? And why? What good would any of their deaths have done her, much less her brother? None of it made any sense.

"What kind of scooter does he have?"

She shook her head.

She shook her head again, then raised her voice over Kirsten's screams. "You think Kevin committed suicide, don't you?"

Matthews scowled, but at least did not evade her question. "At the moment, it looks that way. But we won't know for sure until the medical examiner is through and we look at all the rest of the evidence. We –"

There was a commotion on the porch and the door flung open. Damien, looking as if he'd just climbed out of bed and thrown his clothes back on, shouldered his way towards Mel. Her heart lurched the moment she saw him. *Oh, no.*

He scanned the room, his worried gaze stopping at her and Kirsten. "Are you okay?" he demanded.

Susan Haskell

She wanted to scream NO; she wanted him to rush over and wrap her and Kirsten gently in his arms. Instead, she nodded her head up and down wordlessly. She was okay, or as okay as she'd be until Damien found out *who* the dead man on her doorstep was and what he'd likely done.

He held her gaze for a moment as if assuring himself of her safety, then turned to Matthews. "What have you got?"

"You saw the body?"

He nodded.

"Recognize him?"

"No."

Matthews made a face. "We found the bullet that hit you the other night. It's from the same Colt .45 that killed Ryan and Tony."

He paused, glanced at Mel, then back at Damien. "The semi-automatic found by tonight's vic is the right make. We'll know later if the gun belonged to our shooter."

Damien scowled. "You think tonight's victim is the killer?"

"Could be."

Mel blanched. She knew what was coming now and she'd rather not be here when Damien learned the truth. "Excuse me. I'm going to try to put Kirsten to bed again."

Holding the crying child, she retreated to the bedroom.

~ ~ ~

When the door shut after Mel, Dan turned to Damien. "You don't recognize the guy?"

Damien frowned. "With the black clothing, he could be the guy who shot me. But with the forensics team around him, I didn't get a good look."

He automatically surveyed the small cottage before returning his attention to Dan. The one-room kitchen and living room held shabby but neat furniture, and the bedrooms were right off the living room. Small but typical Key West serviceable.

His former partner came right to the point. "The victim is your bouncer's brother."

"My bouncer?" For a second the words didn't compute.

Then Dan jerked his head in the direction of the hallway down which Mel had just disappeared and the awful truth punched Damien in the gut.

"It's Kevin Saunders. Melissa Saunders' brother. And her roommate is knocked up with the guy's baby."

~ ~ ~

Mel put her ear to the bedroom door. She couldn't hear anything. Had everyone left? It had taken a long time to get Kirsten to go back to sleep. She hoped she'd stay asleep for at least a couple of hours.

She sighed and rested her hot forehead against the cool Dade County Pine of the door. With all the people in such a tiny space and the open door, the window air conditioner just couldn't keep up.

She didn't want to face Damien. Not now. Not after he'd learned that the dead man was not only her brother, but had probably murdered Tony and Ryan too. Not when her attempt at a carefully constructed world had been turned upside down once again. Not when conflicting emotions of sorrow, disbelief, shame and guilt savagely tore at her guts.

She straightened and took a deep breath. She couldn't hide in the bedroom forever. She had to face whoever and whatever was out there, and accept the consequences, no matter what they were or how they hurt her and Kirsten.

She opened the door and walked in to the brightly lit kitchen. Morning light, bright and sunny streamed through the French doors and the small windows into the living and eating nook in the galley kitchen. Joanie was asleep on the couch, and Damien and Matthews sat at the table, quietly talking.

If she'd had any hopes that the news wouldn't affect Damien's attitude to her, they died the moment he turned to look at her. The concern burning in his brown eyes when he arrived had gone out. It had been replaced with an almost unbearable remoteness. Everything inside her cringed, but she did her best to hide it. She held her head high and forced every bit of expression from her face.

Susan Haskell

Matthews stood up, his bald head shining in the bright light. "We're finished here. As soon as we find out more about your brother and how he died, I'll let you know. In the meantime, if you remember anything else of interest about Kevin, you can –"

"I know," she interrupted. "I'll call you."

He glanced at Damien. "You coming?"

"In a minute."

Matthews nodded and left. As his footsteps echoed on the walkway, a stilted silence fell. Mel couldn't think of anything to say that would make any difference, that would offer any comfort that would even begin to bridge the chasm that yawned between them.

Finally Damien looked at his watch. "It's after six already," he said. "Don't bother coming into work tonight."

"It's okay. I can –"

His savage look stopped her dead. He shot up out of his chair, his hands fisted at his sides, his face a mask of pain and anger. "Why didn't you tell me that Joanie was your brother's girlfriend?"

Before she could explain, he cut her off. "Just think real hard if you want to be there tonight."

She wanted to protest, wanted to do anything that would remove the betrayal burning in his eyes.

But before she could collect herself enough to respond, it was too late. The door slammed and he was gone.

Chapter Thirteen

By the next day, Mel's numbness had coalesced into bitter resentment and an aching sorrow for the brother who was a stranger and now was lost to her forever. Everyone, Damien included, had already tried and convicted Kevin for the murders of Tony and Ryan, although they hadn't been able to explain his suicide quite so easily.

Stung by their attitudes, and desperate to get away from Joanie's constant crying, Mel had pestered Matthews for the address of the trailer where Kevin had stayed. Kirsten in a carrier on her back, she sweetly cajoled the landlord into letting her into the trailer to gather up any personal effects – something, anything, that would give her insight into his state of mind, into what he had or hadn't done.

After all the years spent apart, after all the distance, she wasn't sure why she cared. All she knew was that she did. All she knew was that in the end, family is family, whether you like it or not. Blood ties you together whether you like it or not.

Now as she looked around his small, unkempt living room, with the dirty mattress, broken furniture and stale air, her heart sank. Had she really been foolish enough to think she'd find some clue, something the police had overlooked, that would prove his innocence? Something she could wave in front of Damien's face and say "So there!"

Except for an old twenty-inch TV/DVD combo in the corner, and a few clothes on the floor, none of which she recognized, there was little of any value, and nothing that revealed anything about the boy she had once known, or the man he had become. Not a picture, a key chain, a ring, a receipt for groceries or beer, nothing.

A color brochure lay open on the filthy dining table. While Kirsten babbled happily and kicked her bare feet against Mel's back, Mel studied it. Full color pictures of

Susan Haskell

tanned, fit people with perfect teeth smiled back at her from the sunny shores of Venice Beach and Marina del Rey.

She dropped the brochure in disgust. California? Was that his dream? Would she ever know? Shaking her head, she pulled out four drawers one by one. Two were empty, one held a pair of ripped and faded jeans, while three unmatched socks were the only occupants of the bottom one.

She slammed the last drawer shut and stood up. Why had she even bothered to come here? Her gaze toured the room one last time, then she headed for the door. She'd return later this week without Kirsten to pick up the TV.

At the door, she turned back. She decided to see if there was a DVD in the TV's built-in player. Slowly, she crossed the room, and ejected it.

The printed label identified it as *X-Men*. But it was the magic marker lettering that caught her attention. The childish printing had faded, but she remembered it as if they'd written it yesterday. *To Kevin, Love Mel and Darla*, followed by a circle of crooked *X*s and *O*s.

She'd been eleven, Darla was six, and they'd spent weeks collecting soda cans to save for that movie for Kevin's birthday.

Tears started to well in her eyes when another, more painful memory crowded out the first. Kevin, just turned thirteen, his sandy hair long even then, jeans slung low on his rail-thin body. Kevin, inserting himself between her and the punishing blows of yet another one of the long line of deadbeats who had paraded through their mother's bed. And for his efforts to protect her and Darla, suffering a beating that had left his face and body a bruised and bloody pulp. My Kevin.

A sob rose to her lips but she bit it back. She dug her nails mercilessly into her palms. Had that boy, the brother who had fought so hard for her and Darla, turned into a killer? All the years of separation, all her doubts, all her anger at his lifestyle and criminal choices, couldn't convince her it was true.

The question was, what was she going to do about it?

~ ~ ~

Joanie's quiet weeping grated on Mel's nerves, exacerbating the headache that had started before they'd even arrived at the funeral home where they had been such a painfully short time ago. Joanie's crying had continued through the perfunctory service for Kevin and into the reception and showed no sign of stopping anytime soon.

Mel poured herself a cup of coffee and headed to the table where Joanie sat head in hands, shoulders shaking with muffled sobs. In fact, Joanie had done little but cry since Kevin was found shot dead outside their door. Mel had done everything she could think of to console her, including taking over most of the care of Kirsten. But now she'd had enough. Exhausted from worry, from wracking her brains for answers to Kevin's guilt or innocence, figuring how to fit in the temporary shifts she'd picked up yesterday at Russian Delights, she needed the crying to stop.

As calmly as she could, she said, "Stop crying, Joanie. Please, just stop."

Joanie raised a swollen, tear-stained face. She sniffed. "You don't care at all, do you? Your brother's dead, and you could care less."

Mel placed her hand over Joanie's. "That's not true. If you'd only t--"

Joanie yanked her hand away. "Don't touch me. It's all your fault that Kevin's dead anyway." Joanie's voice rose above the voices of the dozen or so people who had come for the funeral.

"What? Lower your voice." The only person that Mel cared about wasn't here, but Mel wasn't interested in putting on a show for Detective Matthews or the few mourners that she knew.

"I don't care who hears." Joanie's voice rose and she shook with anger. "It's your fault that he's dead. If you hadn't hated him so much, he wouldn't have had to sneak around to see me. He would have been able to stay overnight . . ."

She dissolved into a new barrage of tears.

Mel stared at her in shock. Tentatively she touched her shoulder, but Joanie grabbed her hand, flung it away, and wiped at her eyes.

"What?" Mel asked incredulously. "Kevin came to see you?"

"Yes. While you were at work."

Mel rubbed her throbbing temples. "When did this start?"

"About a month ago."

"Why?" Mel couldn't keep the surprise out of her voice.

Joanie fisted her hands on the table and glared at her through her tears. "Because he loved me. Something you wouldn't understand. He realized that he shouldn't have left me. He wanted our baby. After the baby was born, we were going to go out west, to the coast somewhere, start over."

She sniffed again. "Kevin was into something big. He wouldn't tell me what it was, but he was going to make a lot of money. And then we were going to take off with the baby."

Something big. A lot of money. The words went off like shots in Mel's head. Was that what the California brochure she found in his trailer was all about? And how could she have been so blind not to notice the recent changes in Joanie? Her depression had lifted, and she had cleaned and cooked and cared for Kirsten, sometimes even humming and laughing while she worked, a real change from the first couple of months after Kevin had left her.

But no. She'd been too tied up in herself, in her job; in a stupid flirtation with a man who believed her capable of the worst... She sighed. *Stupid, stupid, stupid.*

She glanced up. Across the small room, Matthews sat alone at one of the other tables, a cup of coffee in front of him. But he wasn't looking at the coffee. He was looking at her and Joanie. As were all the other people in the room, including the two guys standing by the rusted coffee urn who pretended to be deep in conversation as soon as they realized she had noticed them eavesdropping.

Mel lowered her voice and leaned closer to Joanie. "Did you tell the police any of this?"

Blood Ties in Key West

"The cops? Are you kidding?" Joanie looked at her as if she'd lost her mind. "They don't care who killed Kevin."

Mel winced. She understood the sentiment. She felt the same. But maybe, if the police knew that Kevin had been visiting Joanie, they might start investigating his death as a homicide, rather than dismissing it as the suicide of a guilty killer. She didn't care if the admission cast more suspicion her way. Despite what Damien and his friend thought, she had nothing to hide.

She looked up at Matthews. Her eyes met his cool, assessing gaze, and somehow she managed not to flinch.

She lifted her chin. "Detective Matthews," she said loudly, "Joanie has something to tell you."

~ ~ ~

Damien had tried to put everything into perspective. He'd really tried. But no matter how he twisted and turned events, he was left with one inescapable fact; he'd just gone to bed with the sister of the man who more likely than not killed his brother and Ryan, and tried to kill him too. And what Dan was telling him now left little room for doubt.

He scrubbed his hands over his face and massaged his tense neck muscles, then looked at Dan. "Are you sure?"

Dan didn't waver. "All the physical evidence points to Kevin Saunders. The bullets that killed Tony and Ryan and wounded you all came from the same gun, the one found lying beside Saunders' body. Some lawyer in New Town reported it stolen early last month."

"Lawyer? Anyone I'd know?"

"Probably not. He's does civil litigation, not criminal law. Name's Jim Findley."

The name sounded familiar to Damien, and Key West being such a small island, it was pretty easy to know most of the local lawyers by name if not by face. "Findley hung out with Tony a few years back, while they were in high school and when he was still managing the club."

But right now Damien didn't care. What he wanted to know was how Kevin Saunders came to be lying dead outside Mel's door. For a moment he thought about how awful it must have been for her to find her brother dead on her doorstep. As awful as it had been for him to see Tony's body at the club. Pity he didn't want to feel welled up inside him but he pushed it aside.

"What about Saunders?" he demanded. "Was it suicide?"

"It looks that way. Saunders' prints are on the gun and there's gunpowder residue on his hand. Looks like he shot himself right through the heart." He grimaced, raising his eyebrows and shook his head.

Damien knew Dan well enough to recognize doubt when he saw it. "But you're not sold?"

"No," he admitted. "Except for the knifing, the circumstantial evidence all fits, but it's a little too neat and tidy for my liking. I hate to say this, but it doesn't feel right. Yeah, Saunders might have wanted to get back at you for running his business out of the club, and for ending up in jail. But why kill Tony and Ryan? Maybe Tony was a mistake, but not Ryan. Not if Saunders was as good a shot as he was supposed to be. And why kill himself?"

Damien frowned. "You guys found the scooter yet?"

Dan shook his head.

"You know, it wasn't just Tony and Cristina who used to go to Shooters N Scooters where Saunders worked," Damien mused. "Their whole group of friends were into it for a while. Started up in their teens."

"Hmm." Dan's eyes narrowed. "Wanna give me the names of those friends?"

"That Jim Findley you mentioned, Alonzo Salva, Esteban Maduro." He rhymed off the names of several other guys and a couple of women. "You'll have to talk to Cristina to get any more names."

"I'll do that." Dan paused. "There's something else that makes me wonder about this alleged suicide."

"Yeah?"

"I went to Saunders' funeral today. Same funeral home as Ryan Ronson. Had an interesting conversation with the sister's roommate Joanie Fisher. The one carrying Saunders' kid."

Damien nodded.

"According to her, he had been visiting her the night of his death. He'd left maybe ninety minutes before the sister came home."

"Did Mel know this?"

Dan hesitated. "I don't think so. She looked pretty pissed off. But then she'd looked pretty miserable through most of the funeral too. Apparently Joanie had been seeing Kevin Saunders behind the sister's back, because she knew she'd object. Kevin had told her he was into something big, something that would bring him a lot of money, and they'd leave for the west coast after the baby was born."

Could Mel have known? Damien wondered darkly. She'd gone to great lengths to tell him that she'd cut her brother off, but was it true? Was anything she'd told him true?

He looked at Dan. "This money thing. D'you think it was some kind of payoff for killing Tony and me? But why? I mean, who benefits if we're both dead? Only Cristina. I don't like Cristina – I never have – but I know she loved Tony. And I can't believe she'd try to have me killed. She's never done anything criminal in her life."

Suddenly he remembered the affair Cristina had confessed to him a few nights ago. With Saunders' death, he'd forgotten all about it.

"But there is something else you can pursue with Cristina." He filled Dan in on the details. "She wouldn't tell me who it was."

Dan nodded and pushed his half-finished soda away. "Your bouncer working tonight?"

Damien didn't have to ask whom Dan meant. He was alternately furious with Mel for luring him in and himself for being lured. Furious that he'd imagined an intriguing depth of tenderness he now knew didn't exist. And furious too, because in spite of everything that had happened, he still wanted her in his bed.

"She'll probably show up."

Dan stood. "Keep an eye on her. I'm not convinced she has anything to do with the murders, or even with her brother, for that matter. But it can't hurt to watch her."

Damien stood too. *Oh, he'd watch all right.*

~ ~ ~

One look at Damien's hard, unforgiving features convinced Mel that she'd reached the right decision after Kevin's funeral earlier in the day.

She'd have to quit her job at Viva Zapata, and she'd have to do it now. Russian Delights had promised her three nights a week starting next Friday. Between that and whatever temp security work she could pick up, she'd just be able to cover the rent, food and transportation for the next month.

It wasn't great, but it was better than staying here. She'd been at Zapata's for only thirty minutes, but she'd already had enough of the polite condolences bar and wait staff made to her face, followed by speculation behind her back about whether her brother killed Tony and Ryan. More than one conversation died as she approached, the furtive looks and intense talk replaced by artificially bright smiles and good cheer.

Worst of all was the way Damien looked right through her, his black eyes icily remote, his mouth taut and grim. She realized then just how much she'd been harboring the secret hope that somehow, some way, he would still want her; still admire her, still care for her. Foolish, dumb hope. She'd learned a lot over the years, but clearly not enough. Not enough that she couldn't be betrayed by her stupid faith in other people. Faith that Joanie was telling the truth. Faith that Damien saw her for who she really was.

She straightened against the bar and clenched her fists. Damien would likely see her quitting as an admission her brother was guilty, and by association, that she was guilty, too. But she couldn't worry about that. She *wouldn't* worry about that.

"Are you all right?"

Becky's shout over the music jarred her back to her surroundings. "What? Oh, yeah, I'm fine."

The waitress frowned. "You don't look fine. Are you sure you should have come back to work this soon?"

Mel took a deep breath and studied Becky. Worry creased her forehead and puckered her mouth. She looked sincere – maybe she was sincere – but what did it matter? Once again she'd learned the hard way it was best not to trust anyone.

"I'm fine," she said quietly, "but I won't be working here any longer. I'm quitting tonight."

"You don't need to leave, Mel. You didn't –"

Mel cut her off. "Do you think my brother killed Tony and Ryan?"

Becky colored. "It doesn't matter what I think, does it?"

Mel smiled sardonically. There was her answer. She pushed away from the bar and headed towards the closed office door. Best to get the resignation over and done with.

She rapped on the door, then pushed it open and made her way inside. The light from the lamp on the desk cast long shadows across the room.

Damien sat at the desk, his fingers poised over his laptop. The soft, yellow light illuminated the dark growth of beard on his jaw, the circles under his black eyes. The eyes that stared at her coldly.

Ignoring the stabbing hurt of that look, Mel made her way to the desk. She stood and looked down at him. It was impossible to believe she'd lain in his arms only four short days ago.

She pushed away the memories and the flare of heat that came with them. "I came in to tell you that I'm quitting. I'll finish out the night and that's it."

Damien's hostile expression didn't change.

Anger flared within her. "I don't care what you or anyone else thinks. You're not the only one who's lost a brother. And I don't believe Kevin killed Tony or Ryan!"

Damien's black eyes flickered. "Are you finished?"

New hurt flooded over her. Damn him, how could he be so cold, so judgmental? Especially after what had passed between them. But then again, everything in her life was a lie; why shouldn't their brief fling be too? Clenching her fists, she swung around and started for the door.

"No."

The hope she hadn't quite managed to kill flared anew. She turned back. "What?"

Every controlled line of his face radiated animosity. "You're staying until I find a permanent replacement. Understand?"

The hope shriveled, killed once and for all. She stood tall and tossed her head.

"Then you'd better have a replacement by next Friday. That's when my new job starts."

Chapter Fourteen

By the end of the night, Damien knew he couldn't let Mel leave until he'd confronted her. What was her new job? Why did she believe her brother was innocent? What else was she holding back from him? It was either get the answers or drive himself crazy.

While he checked the chairs for items patrons had left behind, she came out of the back hall, a black jacket slung over her arm. Her expression was closed, but she still walked with that confident swagger that had intrigued and taunted him from the start. What was she really hiding behind those cool green eyes, inside that tightly controlled body?

"Saunders, you're helping me close up."

Mel glared at him. "I've checked everything. You don't need me for anything else."

The blaze in her eyes and her belligerent stance set his blood boiling in ways that had nothing to do with seeking answers, and everything to do with his overwhelming desire for her. His groin stirred and it was all he could do not to groan aloud.

He gritted his teeth. "You're wrong. I want answers."

"I already told the police everything I know."

"Did you?"

She stiffened. Her hands clenched at her sides. "I'm leaving, Damien."

She moved to sidestep him, but he countered, then swung her around until her back hit the wall. He held her arms hard against the wall, his face only inches from hers. Her weight shifted tellingly, and he tensed in preparation for her defensive move.

To his surprise, she went absolutely still.

He frowned, and his grip on her arms loosened. "You were going to knee me. Why didn't you?"

Her gaze, still wary, met his. "I don't want to hurt you. You've been hurt enough."

He snorted. "If that's true, why didn't you tell me that your roommate was pregnant with your brother's baby? Why did I have to find it out from Dan?"

"It wasn't any of your business."

"No? And what about all that crap you fed me about cutting off your brother? That wasn't true, was it?"

The patience she'd shown up to now disappeared. She lifted her chin. "I don't have to answer your questions, Damien. Move aside and --"

Like a heat-seeking missile, his mouth came down on hers demanding answers she refused to give, seeking to spark in her the same hunger that raged in him. The hunger for truth, hunger for satisfaction, hunger for an end to his frustration with her, with himself and with his life.

Her lips met his, first in shock, then in a brief battle to defend, a battle he knew he had won as soon as her tongue gave way to his and allowed him full entry to the warmth of her mouth.

His hands rose up her arms to her throat, and then tangled in her hair, pulling her closer, deepening the kiss, but it still wasn't enough. He cupped her buttocks, then grappled with the clasp of her slacks. He wanted all of her, naked, now.

Suddenly he was aware of a hand on his wrist, restraining. She dragged her mouth out from under his. "Damien, no!"

"Yes." He claimed her lips once more but she wriggled away from him.

"No. Not like this. You don't want it. I don't want it."

The distress in her voice doused his lust as effectively as a bucket of ice-cold water. He pulled away, then groaned and slid down the wall to the floor.

A moment later, he felt her slide down the wall to the floor beside him. She sat there quietly, not touching him. He didn't look at her. He didn't want to think about what he'd just done.

Finally, when he caught his breath, he said, "I'm sorry. I was out of line."

"Yeah."

He turned his head. In the harsh, bright light, she looked straight ahead, her lips still wet and lush from their kisses, but her face pale and tired. At that moment she didn't look like a tough, no-nonsense bouncer. She looked younger than her twenty-five years, more like a kid, a young woman who, he realized with a jolt, now had no one left in her immediate family except a ten-month-old niece who was more of a responsibility than a comfort. And a roommate who, if Mel was to be believed, had betrayed her.

"Tell me the truth," he said quietly. "Do you think your brother did it?"

This time she turned to look at him, her green eyes wide and filled with a pain he'd never seen in her before. "I want to say no. Everything I remember from our childhood together makes me say no. He . . . . Darla and I idolized Kevin. He was the big brother who protected us. He . . ."

Her voice trailed off for a moment. She cleared her throat. "And the suicide – I just can't accept that. I won't, no matter what the evidence says."

"But you want the truth don't you?"

"The truth is, I don't know *what* my brother might have done or why. In the last thirteen years, I haven't seen him more than a dozen times, and except for Ryan's funeral, not at all since he got out of prison. I don't know him well enough to know what he might or might not have done."

The honesty of her response touched a chord within him. More gently, he pressed on. "Can you think of any reason why he would want to kill Tony and me? And Ryan, for that matter?"

She sighed and shook her head. "Revenge? Money? I'm sure Matthews told you what Joanie said about Kevin being onto something big that would bring him a lot of money. But I don't know, and if Joanie knows, she's not telling."

He took her hand, and laced his fingers through hers. He liked her hands. Slim, with long fingers, and squared-off, unpolished nails. Beautiful, feminine hands, but also nononsense, capable hands not afraid of hard work. He stroked her fingers. Much like the rest of her. Beautiful, but feisty.

He lifted his eyes to hers. For a moment he studied the dark, green depths. Depths that swirled with past secrets he could only imagine, of strengths and desires he had already tasted. And shards of pain and unhappiness that cut into her still.

He tightened his grip on her hand. " Did you have anything to do with those killings, any inkling they were about to happen?"

Her gaze did not flinch from his, but she moistened her bottom lip with her tongue. "Will you believe what I tell you?"

"I want to believe you," he said. "But I need to hear it from you."

"I had nothing to do with it. Any of it. And I can't believe Kevin had . . ." Her voice trailed off and she looked away.

God help him, but he believed her. He wasn't sure why. Maybe it had something to do with Dan's doubts and his own. But he found it impossible to reconcile the murders and the attempt on his life with Mel. He'd seen too much inside her, too much pain and suffering, too much responsibility, too much hunger to be part of decent society, to believe it possible. Maybe he was a fool, but he'd take that chance.

He tugged at her hand until she looked at him. "You should know that Matthews isn't entirely sold on Kevin's guilt either. The circumstantial evidence is there, but that's about it."

She frowned. "Then who does he think did it?"

"That's just it. I don't know about Ryan's death, but the only one who benefits from Tony and my deaths is Cristina. And maybe, a cousin who'd get a small part of the business."

He shook his head. "But Cristina? It's not possible."

Mel's expression was cautious, but he could almost see the wheels turning in her head. Cristina had attacked her physically and verbally. It wouldn't be much of a leap to see her as a killer too.

"I'm not naive," Damien said in response to her unasked question. "Especially when it comes to Cristina. I've known her too long. And I do know she loved Tony. Still loves him. No, it's got to be someone else. We're missing something in this puzzle. I just don't know what it is."

His hand tightened on hers. "You don't need to quit, you know. We could try to figure this out together."

She pulled her hand back. "I need to leave, Damien. I can't stay here. You know it. I know it."

Her determined gaze met his. "But I want to find out who killed my brother – and yours. Anything I find out – anything you find out – we can work together on."

He moved to kiss her, but she held up a hand to ward him off. "There can't be any of this, either."

"This? What do you mean, *this*?"

She smacked his hand away. "You know exactly what I mean. Us. Sex. Together. It just won't work."

He started to object but she continued on brutally. "Even if . . . if the murders hadn't happened, it still wouldn't work between us. We're too different. My world isn't yours, and we both know it."

He didn't try to dissuade her. Not now. There were too many other things to resolve.

But that didn't mean he agreed.

Or that he didn't plan on pursuing her once his brother's murder was resolved once and for all.

~ ~ ~

Damien knew that Dan had asked Cristina about details of the affair from the harsh tenor of her voice on the phone the next day. She didn't allude to their conversation, but he could tell from her dismissive attitude that she was furious he'd revealed her secret. Her tone a weird combination of ice and outrage, she demanded a meeting to discuss the divvying up of the Flores businesses now that it was clear who was behind the murders.

Damien agreed. Despite his doubts about the identity of the murderer, it wasn't Cristina, and there was no reason to put the decision off. He wasn't sure if his sister-in-law was up to a calm, rational discussion of what was to be done, but it was worth a try.

He had planned to take Cristina straight to his office the moment she arrived at Viva Zapata, but his hopes died the moment he saw her walk through the door on the arm of Esteban Maduro. The fact that Maduro wore a suit and carried a briefcase did not bode well for an informal talk to explore the issues for which he had hoped.

His stomach churning, Damien walked over to meet them. He ignored Maduro's smirking presence and nodded at Cristina. Her blonde hair was knotted at the back of her head, and she looked fresher and less tired than she had the last time he'd seen her. She wore a short pink sundress in a style more suited to a young teenager than a woman in her late twenties. Was this a ploy to make her seem more innocent, more helpless, and more needy of his help?

Suppressing a grimace, he greeted her. "I'd hoped we could talk alone."

Cristina started to say something, but Maduro's nasal voice mowed over her. "Forget it, Flores. Cristina's already been sucked dry by one Flores brother. I'm not letting you rip her off as well. I'm here to protect her interests – something you certainly won't do."

What the hell was Maduro talking about? Tony sucking Cristina dry? Even Cristina looked taken aback by his words. Maduro drew his arm around her protectively, as if he were warding off an evil spirit.

The image grated on Damien's nerves, along with Maduro's words. Friend or not, Damien had no doubt Maduro would be collecting a hefty fee from Cristina once a settlement was reached. Hell, he'd probably try to collect it from *him*.

Being one of those perfect Spring Key West days, Damien led Cristina and Maduro to an empty table at the front of the courtyard hoping the ocean breeze would keep all of them cool and calm. Clearly the idea of feeling Cristina out, trying to figure out what would work for both of them, was out of the question now. He wasn't about to make any concessions, any promises, with that barracuda present.

Once they settled back into their chairs, Cristina and Maduro facing Damien across the table, he signaled to Becky to take their order "Beer? Glass of wine?" he asked.

Becky nodded at Cristina when she reached the table. "How are you?" Makeup hid the last pink blotches from Tony's attack with the coffee, but if Cristina remembered, she didn't let on.

Cristina smiled at the familiar face. "Much better now that the guy who killed Tony is dead. It won't bring Tony back, but at least we know who did it, and he's paid for it."

Her words jarred Damien. As soon as Becky took the orders and left, he asked, "How well did you know Kevin Saunders?"

She shrugged. "Not well. I told you we met him at Shooters N Scooters years ago. He's the one who got Tony into coke. He was selling out of here too until Ryan kicked him out and he got busted on some drug charge. By the time he got out of prison, Tony was in rehab."

"You saw Saunders recently?"

"No. I know you don't believe it, but Tony really was trying to stay clean. Saunders called once or twice, a few weeks ago, but Tony told him to stay away from him."

"So why would he want to kill Tony or Ryan? And me?"

"Who knows?" Cristina's bland expression and shrug said she didn't care either. "From what Tony said, Saunders' brains were fried from all the drugs anyway. Who knows how guys like that think? Maybe he blamed you for ruining his life by being run out of the club".

She smiled maliciously. "It wouldn't be the first time you've ruined someone's life."

Damien stiffened. No matter what had happened, no matter what she said, Cristina still blamed him for everything that had gone wrong, right up to Tony's death. She took cheap shots any chance she got.

Becky arrived at that moment with a tray of drinks. It was a good thing. He took a long swig of beer to steel himself to continue.

But before he could say anything, Cristina slammed down her wine glass. "What's wrong with you, Damien?" Her voice rose in indignation. "After her brother killed Tony? After he almost killed you? She was probably in on it too."

Damien followed Cristina's gaze to where Mel patrolled the far side of the club. His hand tightened on his beer glass. "She —"

"Weren't you shot outside her house?" Maduro interrupted, his lizard eyes glittering with excitement from the folds of his chubby face.

He gulped his beer, then smiled gleefully and turned to Cristina. "Looks to me like your brother-in-law has something going with the sister of Tony's killer."

Cristina paled. "Is that true?"

Damien hung on to his temper. "Mel Saunders is a good bouncer," he said flatly. "She didn't have anything to do with Tony's murder."

"Except for throwing him out the door," muttered Cristina.

He glared at her. "If you're worried about her hanging around Tony's beloved club, you can forget it. She's already quit. She'll be gone in a few days."

Cristina railed at him as if she hadn't heard a word he'd said. "I can't believe you'd go out with her, Damien. Not after all that's happened."

"Look, you didn't come here to talk to me about her. You came about the club. What is it you want?"

For a moment Cristina lowered her eyes, then she looked up at him. "Are you going to fight me for Tony's share of the business?"

Damien sighed heavily as he leaned forward. "I don't want to. It was mama's idea to keep Tony's half from him until he proved he was clean. Now that he's dead —" he looked at Cristina pointedly — "and believe me, I know how hard he tried to stay clean — I don't see a reason to —"

Blood Ties in Key West

"Good." Maduro leaned across the table. "I'll have an independent auditor value the business. Cristina will settle for half in cash."

"Cash?" Damien sat back. "You know I'm not going to be able to raise that kind of money. Not without selling everything."

"That's your problem, Flores."

"What do you mean, his problem?" Alonzo Salva hovered over the table. Damien hadn't been that glad to see his lawyer in a long time.

"Seems to me you're getting ahead of yourself, Esteban," Alonzo continued. He looked from him to Cristina, his eyes narrowing. "And not doing what's best for your client, either."

Damien hailed Becky, and signaled for her to bring over a beer for Alonzo. He took the seat across from Esteban.

Alonzo made small talk until his beer arrived, inquiring after everyone's health and the nature of the club's weekend entertainment. He took a long pull from his frosted beer, then shoved his glass aside and placed his palms on the table. He looked hard at Maduro.

"Let's get this straight. First of all, you haven't contested the will yet. Yeah, fifty per cent was supposed to go to Tony if he cleaned up. But he's dead now, and we also know he was still into drugs. It's my opinion no judge would compel Damien to give Tony's widow half. Something of course, but not half."

Without giving Esteban a chance to respond, he went after Cristina. "I know you dislike Damien. But he and I have talked, and he's willing to give you a generous piece of the pie. He's even changed his will to benefit you. If anything happens to him, everything goes to you. I don't think this is a man you want to bleed dry, especially not for short term gain."

Damien blinked. He'd changed his will? He and Alonzo had *talked* about changing his will, but it hadn't happened yet. And wouldn't until they had worked out some kind of deal. But he kept his mouth shut. So far, Alonzo was handling this far better than he had.

~ ~ ~

Kirsten's giggles were balm to Mel's soul as she chased her around the coffee table in the living room on a sunny afternoon a couple of days later. The ten-month-old couldn't walk yet, but she could crawl across the combination living room and kitchen in a heartbeat. Her favorite game was to lead Mel on all fours around the room. Whenever Mel came within striking distance, Kirsten would put on a burst of speed and scuttle to a new area of the room, crowing with delight.

Finally, tired of the game, Mel picked the child up. She looked down at her chubby little face, with the blue eyes and dark lashes so like her sister's, and the beautiful rosebud mouth, and smiled sadly. Her sister had once been a similar tiny bundle, full of life and potential, but it had come to naught, snuffed out by her own carelessness and an abusive man's angry fists. Much like Kevin's life had ended, in a puddle of his blood, outside her door.

She hugged Kirsten tightly to her, and the child squawked in objection. She would never, ever, let anything like that happen to Kirsten. She didn't know how she'd do it, or even *if* she could do it, but she *would* do it. She loosened her grip on the baby and jiggled her until she giggled again. No, no matter what it took, she would see that Kirsten had every chance for a good life.

Kirsten stuck her thumb in her mouth and cuddled closer. The simple, trusting act made Mel's throat tighten. When she saw Kirsten like this, she had to believe that everything would be all right. Yes, Kevin was dead, and she hadn't been able to pry anything out of Joanie that would help prove his innocence. Yes, she would be leaving Viva Zapata in a few days. Yes, she'd probably never see Damien again after that.

A lump rose in her throat as she faced that reality but she forced it down. Her lips grazed Kirsten's forehead, and she sat on the sofa. On the plus side, Russian Delights had just come through with a full-time job, at a better salary than when she'd left. Her brother's alleged murder of two men had given her some kind of weird cachet with the management there.

"I'm going out." Joanie, blotchy-faced and sullen, stood in the kitchen. Her dark brown hair was pulled back from her face in a ponytail. She wore a loose cotton top over maternity jeans and a pair of florescent orange flip-flops. Purse straps dangled from her fingers.

"Where you going?"

"You're not my mother, Mel. Get off my back."

Mel winced. Joanie had finally stopped crying, but she had done nothing but mope around the cottage since Kevin's funeral. Every look, every gesture made it clear she blamed Mel for Kevin's death. Mel had tried to comfort her, tried to convince her to help find Kevin's killer, but Joanie would have none of it. If she wanted Mel to throw herself on the floor and beg for forgiveness for Kevin's death, she could forget it.

Mel held back the angry retort that came to mind. "You'll be back before seven?" she asked.

Joanie shrugged and headed for the door, her flip-flops slapping defiantly on the floor.

~ ~ ~

At six thirty, Joanie still wasn't back. Mel called the Rubensteins in the front cottage, but there was no answer. She called Don and Betty Leeson. The same thing.

At six forty-five, Mel picked up Kirsten and carried her to the house two doors over. Thirteen-year-old Selma Jackson lived there, and she'd watched Kirsten on several occasions when Joanie had gone out with friends on nights when Mel was working.

Her knock on the door was answered by Mrs. Jackson, a thin wiry woman who looked to be in her mid-forties. Wiping her hands on an apron she wore over a tan skirt and blouse, she looked Mel up and down, her gaze stopping momentarily on the baby. Kirsten chose that moment to break into her most winning smile, and the woman smiled back before looking at Mel. "Yes?"

"Mrs. Jackson, I'm Melissa Saunders. Selma has babysat Kirsten a couple of times, and I was hoping she'd be able to come over now for an hour or two, until my roommate gets back. I've got to go to work in a few minutes."

Mrs. Jackson paused. Her smile wavered. "You live on the next block?"

"Yes, in the potter's cottage behind the Rubensteins'."

"The house where the man was found shot dead at the door?"

Mel suppressed a groan. "Yes."

The last vestiges of friendliness disappeared from the woman's face. "Selma is busy."

She started to close the door, but Mel's hand shot out to hold it open. "Please, Mrs. Jackson. I'm desperate. It should only be for an hour or so."

The plea had no effect on Mrs. Jackson. "No. We don't want anything to do with your kind."

Your kind. The words stung as much as having the door slammed in her face a second later.

Her expression grim, Mel marched back home with Kirsten. Joanie still wasn't back. What was she going to do? She glanced at the clock. Five to seven.

She sat Kirsten on the pitted linoleum floor in the kitchen. Delighted to be free, the child crawled a few feet to the coffee table, then hoisted herself up and grinned up at Mel.

Watching the baby, Mel searched for Becky's number. It was her last chance. If she hadn't left for work yet, maybe she knew someone who would take Kirsten for the evening.

Becky picked up on the first ring. "I'm on my way out the door. Make it fast."

"It's Mel. Mel Saunders. I'm in a tight spot, Becky. Is your sister in? D'you think she would watch Kirsten for the evening? I could bring her to your place."

"I'm sure she would, but she's not here. She's working the afternoon shift at Martin's this week. Where's Joanie?"

Mel sighed. "She took off about four this afternoon and hasn't come back. I have a feeling she's not going to, at least not for a while."

Becky paused. "Why don't you bring Kirsten to work with you?"

"To work? Oh, yeah. That'd work. The bouncer with the baby in a back carrier. Not to mention all the laws it probably breaks."

"Hey, it's Key West! I'm serious, Mel. You've got one of those fold-up playpens? Bring that, and put her to bed in Damien's office. Everyone can take turns going in and watching her until she falls asleep."

Mel winced. "Damien will have a fit."

"Does it matter what he thinks? You're leaving."

Becky was right. And she couldn't afford to lose a night's pay.

She said a hurried goodbye, then scooped up Kirsten from her position beside the coffee table, where she was happily ripping a magazine apart.

"Okay, baby, it's time *we* went to work."

Chapter Fifteen

The moment he entered Viva Zapata, Damien made a beeline for his office. Out of the corner of his eye, he saw Becky flagging him down but he ignored her. His cell phone had died and he wanted to get this call out of the way before it got too late.

He yanked open the door, then stopped short.

In front of his desk stood Mel, clothed in her usual form-fitting black clothes, her attractive backside turned towards him. What wasn't usual were the two big round eyes solemnly staring at him from the chubby little face half visible over her left shoulder. The face of a baby. Her baby. Or at least, her baby niece.

Mel whirled around. When she saw him, she blanched. "Didn't Becky tell you? Joanie didn't –"

"Sorry, Mel. He didn't give me a chance." Panting, Becky stepped around Damien. "That's why I was waving you down, Damien. I wanted to tell you about the baby."

Damien looked from Mel to Becky and back. "Well, *somebody* better tell me about the baby."

"I didn't –"

"It was my i–"

Both women stopped. Becky laughed. "I'm sure Mel can explain." She slipped out the door.

"Well?"

The baby squirmed around in Mel's arms to look at Damien too. With her dark curly hair, bright blue eyes and porcelain skin, she could easily have been Mel's daughter. Only her brilliant smile was in contrast to her aunt's sober expression.

"It was an emergency," Mel said quietly. "Joanie didn't come home and I couldn't get any of my usual backups. Kirsten should go to sleep in a few minutes, and then Becky and I will keep checking on her on and off during the night."

Susan Haskell

She didn't ask if it was okay with him but it didn't matter. He was mesmerized by the urchin's winning grin. "She looks like you."   "So if you – what?" Mel frowned. "You know she's not mine. She's my sister's daughter – my half-sister's, at that."

Damien grinned. "Maybe I meant she's just beautiful like you."

That silenced her. She shut her mouth and stared at him. His gaze lingered on her unsmiling lips.

He cleared his throat. "It's okay. About the baby, I mean. I'll do your work until she's asleep, and then I'll come back. In the meantime, I need to ask you a question."

"All right." She wrestled Kirsten back to her shoulder, but the inquisitive child kept trying to turn back to look at Damien.

"It's about Kevin."

She stilled. "Yes?"

"Did Kevin own a scooter?"

She shook her head. "Your friend already asked me that. Kevin didn't own a scooter that I know of." She paused. "Why?"

"The police haven't found anything to indicate he owned a scooter. We don't even know if Kevin's the one who stole that black Zuma from Shooters N Scooters." He lowered his voice. "It didn't occur to me until today, but Tony used to have a scooter, a black Zuma 2-stroke. He bought it after he broke his leg dirt biking." He paused. "Maybe he sold it – I'm sure he hasn't ridden it the last couple of years."

She looked up from Kirsten, her expression carefully neutral. "Can you find out where it is?"

"I can try. I'm not Cristina's favorite person these days, but there's no reason she wouldn't tell me where it is."

She shifted the child in her arms. "If you wouldn't mind leaving for a few minutes, it'll be easier to get Kirsten to sleep. I'll come out and get you as soon as she's down." She nodded at the small playpen pushed up beside the sofa.

Damien left. He'd call Cristina as soon as he had a chance to get back to his office.

It was a good twenty minutes before Mel touched his arm and asked for the headset. He gave it to her, his hand lingering on hers a moment too long. "Kirsten's asleep?"

"For now."

He turned to head towards his office.

She grabbed his arm. "Damien."

He turned to face her.

"I'm sorry. About tonight and Kirsten. About . . . about everything."

His gaze met hers. He knew she wasn't just talking about the baby in his office. He placed his hand over hers and gave a tender squeeze. "I know."

When he reached the office door, he looked back. Mel was still watching him. He raised a finger to his lips to assure her he'd be quiet, then disappeared inside.

Only the light on his desk was on, and it had been placed on the lowest setting. Kirsten lay on her side on a flannel blanket in the middle of the playpen. She wore a turquoise terry sleeper, and a cotton sheet had been pulled up over her.

For several moments Damien stood and watched her. She looked so peaceful, oblivious to the strains and tensions engulfing the adults around her. Her breath came in and out, then she'd start sucking. Beside her lay a soother, rejected in favor of the comfort offered by her own thumb.

Damien smiled and retreated to his desk. Mel or Becky had turned off the ringer on the phone, but the lights would still flash to alert him of any incoming calls, or Gord could pick them up at the bar. He needed to make just one call. He picked up the receiver and punched in the first couple of digits.

The plastic bottom of the playpen crinkled. Kirsten rolled onto her back. Damien set down the receiver. He'd wait another couple of minutes. The minutes passed. The child didn't move or make a sound. He picked the receiver up again. As quietly as he could, he punched in Cristina's number.

Susan Haskell

The phone had barely begun to ring when a high-pitched wail pierced the air. Damien put down the receiver as Kirsten flung off the sheet and her arms and legs flailed about.

He picked up the crying child and retrieved the soother from the far side of the playpen. At first Kirsten rejected the soother, but finally she took it, stopped crying, and settled her warm little body against his shoulder. He stood, bouncing the child slightly, and breathed in her sweet baby scent. His lips grazed the top of her head, and he began to whisper a *cancion de cuna*, surprised that he could still remember the words of his favorite lullaby. "*Arruru mi niña, arrurú mi amor; Arruru pedazo de mi corazón* . . . . go to sleep my little one, my love; go to sleep little piece of my heart."

"You don't have to do that." Mel stood in the doorway.

"I know." He smiled. "It was just a lullaby, one my mother used to sing to Tony and me."

In the dim light, her eyes looked funny, as if she were trying not to cry. "You look good with a baby in your arms."

His gaze held hers and this time the yearning that arced between them was palpable. He smiled wistfully. "I think I look pretty good with the baby's aunt in my arms too."

A flash of anguish crossed her face. She held out her arms. "Let me try to put her down again."

~ ~ ~

Later that night when Damien insisted on sending Mel and Kirsten home early in a cab, Mel was thankful.

When he saw her to the cab, put the playpen in the trunk, and then handed the sleeping child in to her, it was all she could do to utter a few hoarse words of gratitude.

And when he leaned into the window, his muscular forearms on the doorframe, and his brow furrowed with concern, the power of thought and speech left her altogether.

After a moment of silence, he held out a business card.

"Go on, take it." The card fluttered onto the sleeping child's lap. "My home and cell numbers are on it, as well as the club's. If you have any problems getting a babysitter –"

His dark eyes locked with hers. " Or *any* problems at all – I want you to call me. Understand?"

She wanted desperately to make some jaunty retort, some smart-ass comment that would make it clear she didn't need his help – never had, never would – but the best she could come up with was, "Yeah, I'll do that."

Then she leaned forward and gave the cab driver the address. Damien stepped back and the cab pulled away from the curb.

Despite herself, she turned to look back. He stood there still, a tall dark form leaning against one of the pillars in front the club, his hands in his pockets, watching after them. Watching after her.

It was an unsettling feeling.

Abruptly she turned to face the front. Something fluttered to the floor.

It was Damien's business card. With shaky fingers she retrieved it. In the flickering of the streetlights, she looked at the numbers. It would be so easy, it would be such a relief, to call him, to ask for his help, to rely on him as he was clearly asking her to do.

But they were numbers she would never call. *Could* never call. The card crumpled as her fingers closed tightly over it.

~ ~ ~

Joanie hadn't moved from the sofa where Mel had found her fast asleep when she returned home with Kirsten last night. Joanie was awake now, staring dully at *Days of Our Lives*, but hadn't changed her clothes or eaten since yesterday. Kirsten had just gone down for her afternoon nap.

Mel took a seat across the room from her. "Joanie."

The girl continued staring at the TV as if she hadn't heard. Finally Mel stood up, snapped off the television, and sat on the coffee table directly in front of her.

Joanie blinked. "What'd you do that for?"

"This can't go on, Joanie."

"What?"

"You know." Mel leaned forward, her hands on her knees. "Your not being here when I need you. That was the deal when you decided to come live with Kirsten and me. You help me; I help you. You have room and board and spending money and I have a sitter."

Pouting, Joanie turned her head away and rested her chin on a petite fist. "Why should I help you?"

Mel sighed. She already had one child to take care of; she didn't need another. Reining in her exasperation, she continued. "Because I need you. Kirsten needs you." She paused. "And I don't hate Kevin. I hate that he's dead. But –"

"But what?" The mention of Kevin's name sparked the first sign of interest from Joanie, however surly.

Mel had said it all before, but it had to be said again. "You know it would never have worked with Kevin. He was still on drugs, back selling them too. And whatever that "big" thing was he talked to you about, probably wouldn't have been legal. Even if he'd taken you out West like he promised, even if he'd stayed with you and the baby, you know that one day he wouldn't have come home. Maybe he'd be arrested; maybe he'd overdosed; maybe he'd be dead. But he'd be gone."

"That's not true." The denial came more slowly this time.

"I wish it wasn't."

"Kevin didn't kill anyone." Joanie's voice rose in a heart-rending wail. "I know he wouldn't do it. And he didn't kill himself either."

Mel wished she had Joanie's certainty. Despite what she'd said to Damien, despite what she wanted to believe of her brother, a part of her still feared the worst. "I don't want to think he killed himself," she said slowly. "Or anyone else, either. I hope he didn't. I really do. So if you know anything – anything at all – that shows he didn't do it – tell me."

Tears welled up in Joanie's eyes and slid silently down her plump cheeks. Despite her pregnancy, she looked small and defeated, and younger than ever.

Mel joined her on the sofa, and awkwardly slid her arm around the young woman. "I just want the best for us,

Joanie. For you and your baby. For Kirsten and me. But I need your help. I can't do it alone. I –"

The doorbell rang, its chimes loud and jarring. Mel eased away from Joanie and stood up. The interruption was annoying, but it was also a relief. Providing comfort wasn't Mel's strong suit.

"I'll be right back."

She strode across the room and flung open the door. "Yes?"

All five-foot-two-inches of her landlord, Mr. Rubenstein, startled at her abruptness. Short and dapper with a well coiffed comb-over, the retired Mr. Rubenstein was usually a model of old-world manners and grace. Mel admired him for his quiet strength and kindness, but mostly because he had taken a long look at Kirsten, Joanie and herself, and taken a chance on them as tenants.

Now, Mr. Rubenstein looked uncomfortable. *More than uncomfortable – decidedly nervous.* He fiddled with a couple of folded sheets of paper and stared at Mel's knees.

"Mr. Rubenstein," she said, belatedly remembering her manners. Then, struck again by how ill at ease he was, she blurted out, "Is something wrong?"

He raised his gentle brown eyes and peered at her over his round wire-rimmed glasses. "I'm afraid there is."

"It's not your wife, is it? Is Mrs. Rubenstein's okay?"

"No. No, nothing like that. Thank you for asking."

She gestured to the sofa. "Would you like to come in?"

"No." He took a deep breath, then raised the papers. "It's about this petition."

"Petition?"

"Yes. The neighbors . . ." He paused to work his mouth around his teeth, as if they no longer fit properly. "The neighbors . . . well, this has always been a quiet street. The shootings – outside our home – and then your brother's sui–"

His face flamed. After a moment, he continued doggedly on, his voice quavering. "Your brother's death right outside your door – that's really shaken them."

"And the petition?" Mel prompted. She had a horrible feeling she knew what was coming.

"Ahem. Yes. The petition. The neighbors brought me this petition yesterday. Everyone on the street has signed it."

Unwilling to help him out, she waited while he fidgeted some more.

Finally, his face reddening again, his voice pleading, he said, "The thing is, the neighbors don't want this kind of violence on our street. They're not used to it."

The awkward silence lengthened.

"They want you evicted."

Chapter Sixteen

So many bad things had happened in the last few weeks that Mr. Rubenstein's statement barely penetrated the wall Mel had erected around herself. She stared at him unblinkingly.

"Did you hear what I said?" he quavered.

"Yes. I heard you." With effort she straightened and erased every shred of friendliness from her face. "We still have eight months left on our lease."

"I know. I know." The little man raised his trembling hands, rustling the folded papers that carried the latest bad news. "But we've lived here for forty-five years and never had any trouble with tenants. I don't want trouble now."

He was so upset Mel had trouble maintaining her harsh defense. But she had to, for Kirsten, and for Joanie, and for herself. She put her hands on her hips. "I know my rights," she said flatly. "You'll have to take us to court if you want us out."

"Please, Miss Saunders." Mr. Rubenstein's trembling spread, until every part of him was shaking, and the papers in his hands rustled uncontrollably. "We're not young any more. I've got a bad heart. The wife's got high blood pressure and diabetes. This is all too much for us."

The ache behind Mel's eyes grew to thunderous levels. She leveled a fierce stare at her landlord.

But try as she might, it was impossible to see a hardhearted bastard who wanted to toss them out onto the street. What she saw was a frail old man, nearing eighty and she didn't want to be involved in any more deaths. She saw a courtly, kind man who, against all likelihood, had taken a chance and rented the cottage next to his own home to the unlikely tenants of a bouncer, her baby niece, and a pregnant twenty-year-old. A man and his wife, who instead of being put off by the prospect of crying babies and single mothers, had welcomed them with open arms.

Mel wanted to tell him no. Go away. Take yourself and that stupid petition and get out. But the sight of his watery brown eyes, his gnarled hands, the pleading look on his face, undid her.

"I'll start looking for a new apartment next week, okay?" she said gruffly. "But I can't promise how soon we'll be out."

Relief blossomed on the old man's face. "Oh, thank you. Thank you so much." He held the papers out to her. "Do you want to see the petition?"

"No."

~ ~ ~

Damien was in his office in the early evening when the door slammed open and Mel barreled in. Without breaking stride she bore down on him. When she reached his desk, she ripped the pen from his hand, plopped both fists down on the desk and leaned forward until she was nose to nose with him.

"If you didn't want me to come in tonight, why didn't you just say so?"

Green eyes sparked with anger in her flushed face. Under the low-cut black top her chest heaved and the swell of creamy breast rose and fell just below his line of vision. She had never looked more furious, or exuded more raging sexuality.

It took an act of will – or perhaps self-preservation – not to reach for her. Instead, Damien asked, "What are you talking about?"

"The other security guy. Why is he here?"

So that was it. He relaxed marginally. "Sit down and I'll tell you."

"No!" She hurled the word at him. "Tell me why he's here. I have a few more days before I leave."

Carefully he placed one hand over hers, but she yanked it away. For a moment he thought her poised fist was about to connect with his jaw, but she checked herself at the last minute.

"Just tell me what's going on."

He sat back. "All right. There's a job I want taken care of tonight, off-site. It involves your brother and mine. I want your help."

She didn't move. "Yeah? What is it?"

"It's hard to explain when you're glaring at me like you want to throttle me."

"Oh." Slowly she slid back from his desk and straightened, but she didn't sit down. She looked brittle, fragile, and very, very angry, as if one touch, one wrong word, would set off an explosion. Damien had never seen her this upset, not after her brother was killed, not after Cory's death, not even after Tony's death and suspicion had fallen on her.

"Is something wrong?" he asked.

"No." But her body language screamed the opposite; that she'd been pushed to the brink and couldn't take much more.

She raised her chin. "What's this job you're talking about?"

"I was on the phone to Cristina earlier. Seems Tony's Zuma hasn't been sold after all. It's stored where Esteban Maduro lives, at the Key West Beach Club. It's in the garage there, in the same parking space where Maduro keeps his own Suzuki. I believe he's out of town on a case right now, but I'd like to take a look at that scooter."

"Oh." That seemed to take the starch out of her. She frowned. "You said it was black, didn't you?"

"Yes."

Though it was clear she made the connection, she showed no enthusiasm.

"What's wrong?" he demanded again. There had to be something wrong. Was she afraid that what they found would only point more strongly to Kevin? "Don't you want to prove your brother's innocence?"

Light flared in her eyes. "Of course."

She snapped out of the chair and stalked to the doorway. At the door she pivoted to face him. "So when do we leave?"

~ ~ ~

Susan Haskell

As they drove along Atlantic Boulevard, Mel stared at the square dark form of the two buildings comprising the Key West Beach Club condos rising from their lush landscaped surroundings overlooking the Atlantic Ocean. It was only four stories high because of Key West's height restrictions but seemed huge when compared to the places she was used to in Old Town.

She scanned the high cement walls on either side of the closed entry gate as they turned into the well-illuminated driveway. "I hope you don't think I'm going to break into this place for you," she said, the first time she's spoken since they'd headed onto Duval ten minutes ago for Esteban Maduro's condo. Damien hadn't opened his mouth either.

Which was good. She couldn't hold out against him much longer. His questions weren't the problem. It was the concern behind them.

Insults, accusations, anger – she could handle all that. What she couldn't handle was kindness. Kindness would destroy her. In those last moments in his office, she had been that close to falling apart and blurting out the whole sorry mess: Joanie's recalcitrance, the petition to evict them from their home, the momentous hurdle of trying to find another decent, reasonably priced rental that would take two young women and a baby, with another on the way, and still be close to the jobs in Old Town.

Mel would rather go to on Samuel's House for housing and financial support than rely on Damien and his kind. She couldn't afford to fall to pieces now. With the rare exception of her foster parents, the only one she'd ever been able to rely upon was herself. No matter how tempting Damien's arms, she couldn't afford to weaken. One way or the other, she would pay for it later.

Damien reversed the car to reposition it outside the closed white metal entry gates into the property. He put it in park, shut off the headlights and turned to her.

"Neither of us should have to break in," he said quietly. "I'm counting on at least one or two of the residents returning in the next half hour or so. That security gate has individual codes for each unit. When a resident punches in the code to open the gate, we'll be right on his tail. By the time the door closes, we'll be heading to the underground garage."

"Rather sneaky for an ex-cop. Why didn't you just get your friend Matthews to check it out?"

"I'm tired of waiting for someone else to come up with all the answers. The least I can do for Tony now is make sure we pin his death on the right guy."

Mel opened the window. She shivered in the damp, salty breeze even though it was warm. *What if Kevin turned out to be the right guy?*

Except for the incessant frogs croaking behind the walls, the silence lengthened. She had to force herself not to clasp and unclasp her hands, not to squirm about in the seat – not to steal quick looks at Damien. A whiff of his aftershave reached her, something tangy and fresh, and with it came a pang of regret so sharp she almost gasped aloud.

"Joanie come back?"

His question brought her back to the painful awkwardness of the present. She stiffened. "Yes."

"Is it going to be all right? She'll stay?"

"Stop it, Damien." For her own sake, she had to keep pushing him away. "You don't need to know any of this. I'll be gone in a few days and you won't have to think about me again."

"But –"

She cut him off before the hurt in his eyes could touch her. "I'm here, aren't I? That should be enough for you."

"It isn't."

The firm, insistent voice flowed around her, embracing her like a caress.

The flash of headlights flickered in his side mirror. "There's our ticket in," he said. "Let's go."

Damien slowly accelerated after the vehicle heading for the gate. He stopped inches from the back bumper of the orange-colored Honda sedan, while its white-haired driver leaned out her window to punch in the code to open it.

Susan Haskell

When the Honda moved, Damien followed, and they made it inside before the gate had begun to slowly close.

As soon as they were inside, Damien made a hard left at the oversized blue tiled fountain as the Honda turned right. Since he could access the garages from both sides, there was no sense in scaring the driver of the Honda.

"You know which spot is Maduro's?" Mel asked.

"Cristina said it was against the wall on the ocean side, near the middle. His name will be stenciled on the cement parking curb. We'll just have to keep our eyes open for it."

They turned right and entered the low-ceilinged garage which had several security cameras and overhead lighting. They proceeded, scanning the parking curbs in the parking spaces along the back wall.

"There it is. Maduro."

Damien stopped. On one side was parked a green Toyota, on the other a four- person golf cart. Between the two vehicles, in a space stained with oil, stood a cloth-covered scooter. One scooter.

~ ~ ~

After it had sunk in that there should have been two scooters in the space, one belonging to Maduro and one to Tony, Mel asked, "Where's the other one?" She looked at Damien. "Would Maduro have used a scooter for out-of-town business?"

Damien frowned. "I doubt it. We'll park, and come back to see which bike it is."

He pulled into the next empty bay. They got out of the car, took a quick look around for observers, and headed back.

Skirting the oil patches, Damien approached the cloth-covered bike. He undid a couple of ties, then lifted the tarp covering the front end of the bike. As he pulled it back from the front fenders and the handlebars. "*Mierda*," he swore under his breath.

Mel knew little about scooters, but one thing was evident. This one was blue, not black.

Damien yanked the cloth back in place and knelt to secure the ties.

"It's not Tony's, is it?" Mel asked.

Damien stood up. "No. It's a Suzuki. Tony's is a –"

"Flores!"

They both froze.

"*Vete para el carajo*! Get away from my bike!"

Chapter Seventeen

The familiar nasal twang screeched across Damien's nerves. Maduro! The last person he wanted to see.

He rose from his crouching position to face his sister-in-law's lawyer. He noted Mel's menacing expression, and almost smiled. If he needed a bodyguard, she'd be the perfect one to choose.

He turned his attention to Maduro. The younger man wore a white shirt, the collar open and sleeves rolled up, and belted grey dress pants. He'd clearly rushed here from wherever he was working, probably after a call from Cristina.

"Buenas tardes, Esteban," Damien said mildly. "Weren't you supposed to be out of town?"

"You wish," Maduro sneered. He looked as smug as a cat that had just caught a mouse swimming in his bowl of cream. "What are you doing nosing around my bike?"

Damien wasn't the least bit perturbed, and he made sure Maduro could see that. "I'm not interested in your Suzuki. I'm interested in Tony's Zuma. I'm sure Cristina told you that when she called you."

He motioned to the empty space beside him. "And speaking of Tony's bike, where is it?"

"Tony's? It –" Maduro sputtered to a stop. His eyes tracked back and forth and his mouth gaped. For the first time, he seemed to notice there was only one vehicle parked in the space.

After a moment, he regained his composure. He scowled at Mel and then Damien. "All right, what did you do with it?"

"Cut the crap, Esteban. Since you've clearly spoken to Cristina, you know I was thinking of buying it from her. Why would I steal it?"

Taking advantage of Maduro's surprise, he pressed home his point. "So maybe you can tell me, Esteban. Where *is* Tony's bike?"

"I . . . I don't know. It was here the last time I looked."

"And when was that?"

Maduro grimaced. "Maybe two months ago."

"You haven't taken your own bike out for a spin?"

"No. I've been too busy."

"What about your friends? Could one of them have borrowed it?"

Maduro looked more uncomfortable than ever. "I don't know how. The keys are still up in my condo."

"You sure of that?" Damien drawled.

"*Creo que si.* Of course!"

"Yeah. Right. As sure as you were about the bike being here."

Without waiting for a response, Damien pulled his cell out of his pocket.

"What are you doing?"

Damien looked up from the phone. "Calling the police to report a stolen vehicle."

He glanced at Mel, then back at Maduro. "You've got an objection?"

Ashen, Maduro shook his head.

***

The March sunshine bathed Damien in light, gilding his olive skin with a warm golden cast The scent of Cape Jasmine perfumed the air. From nearby came the soothing sound of a rock fountain and the lilting refrain of a birdsong.

A hand at Mel's hip, gently stroking her bare skin, awakened a yearning deep within her. The pulse at her throat quickened, and slowly her eyelids fluttered open.

The heat of Damien's gaze blasted over her in a shock of flame, stealing the breath from her lips and setting off brush fires in every part of her body.

Her lips curved slowly upwards and she leaned towards him, craving his touch, his taste, his body around her, and the promise of searing union in his eyes.

As he reached to claim her, a whine in the distance invaded her consciousness. Swiftly it grew into the wail of a siren, loud and insistent and then . . .

Blood Ties in Key West

Mel jerked upright. Kirsten's piercing screams penetrated the shut door to her bedroom to put a screeching halt to her dream. Blinking, she glanced at the alarm clock. It was only quarter to ten. *Why was Joanie letting her scream like that?*

She threw back the sheet, and swung her feet to the floor. What was wrong with that girl? They'd talked about this before. Especially now, when there were so many problems to figure out, Mel needed at least a few precious hours of sleep a day. It was already hard enough with the roosters crowing at all hours of the day.

Yanking her t-shirt over her panties, she opened the door and padded barefoot to the living room. There was Kirsten, tears streaming down her flushed face, standing and clutching the edge of the playpen.

Mel lifted the crying child out of the playpen. She hugged the hot, sodden little form to her chest. "Hey, sweetie, it's okay, it's okay," she soothed, then wrinkled her nose as the odor of a heavily soiled diaper rose to meet her. "Hey, hey," she said, kissing the top of Kirsten's head. "Is that why you're crying?"

Patting the child, she moved to the sofa, grabbed a changing pad from the arm, and laid it flat on the cushions. As soon as Kirsten stopped crying, she lowered her to the pad and set about changing her diaper. It was a task she did quickly and efficiently now, though she hadn't a clue how to do it when Kirsten had first come into her life.

Once the diaper was secure, Mel tickled Kirsten's toes until the child was cooing and laughing once more. She picked her up, settled her on her hip, and looked around. *Where was Joanie?*

"Joanie?"

The bathroom door, as well as the door to Joanie's room, hung open so she wasn't here. Despite her roommate's failure to return home before Mel had to leave for work the other night, Joanie was usually pretty reliable, especially when it came to Kirsten.

Unless. Mel froze. Could Joanie have gone into labor? Her due date was still two months off. Surely she would have woken her? They'd talked about Mel being with her at the Lower Keys Medical Center for the birth.

Kirsten still on her hip, she went to Joanie's room. What she saw was not encouraging. Two of the drawers gaped crookedly from the dresser. A closer inspection showed they were empty, as were the other two drawers.

With a sinking feeling, Mel crossed the room to the small armoire. A couple of Joanie's pre-pregnancy dresses and several blouses and pairs of pants hung there. Only the maternity clothes were missing.

Slowly she returned to the kitchen. *Joanie couldn't have left.* Where would she have gone? Her older sister had made it clear she wanted nothing to do with Joanie and her baby. Who else could she have gone to?

She scanned the kitchen, her gaze stopping at a scrap of paper beside the coffee maker. She crossed the living room and picked up the paper.

Joanie's lopsided printing stared back at her. "I'm moving out. I'll be back in a couple of days to get my stuff."

Kirsten grabbed for the note. Mel yanked it away from her. "No!"

The child started to cry. She waved her chubby fist at the paper in Mel's hand. Mel crumpled it and threw it on the counter. She hugged Kirsten and rocked her back and forth, hoping to comfort them both.

As the child's cries subsided, the warmth and closeness of the little body propelled Mel back to the sweetness and security of her dream. She shut her eyes, and for a moment she felt once more the wonder and warmth of Damien's love, the protection of his arms, the luxury of knowing she would be safe in his embrace. If only she could rely on his help.

But she couldn't. Her eyes opened. That was a dream, as distant and out of reach as it had always been, probably brought on by the intensive time they'd spent together last night.

Blood Ties in Key West

No, she had to do it herself. The only time it had been different was with her foster parents, but she wasn't a foster kid any more and Don and Betty were retired. They didn't need her bringing her problems home to them.

Any more than Damien – her boss, or about-to-be former boss – needed her asking him for favors. No, she would do it herself.

She took Kirsten into her room, and threw on shorts. She spent the rest of the morning playing with her, crawling after her in the tiny patch of Bahia grass in the backyard and lifting her onto her shoulders for a tour of the flamingo red poinciana tree blossoms, all the while considering options and examining the cost and practicality of her limited choices. They ventured out front for a short walk, only to earn stony glances from a couple of older neighborhood woman chatting with one another.

Mel ignored them. She knew what the neighbors thought. She was moving, wasn't she? What more did they want?

By the time she'd fed Kirsten and put her in her room for an afternoon map, she'd already mapped out a plan. First, she'd make a few calls to try to track down Joanie and convince her to come back, at least until they moved. If that didn't work, she'd have to try Don and Betty. They'd made it clear they'd be happy to take Kirsten in a pinch, but she didn't want to take advantage of their kindness. They'd already done so much for her.

If Joanie wouldn't come back, there'd be a whole new set of problems to face. On the one hand, it would be a lot easier, and cheaper, to find a studio or one bedroom apartment for just Kirsten and herself. But finding a babysitter she could afford was going to be tough – especially with the hours she worked.

She grabbed the old dog-eared phone book that came with the cottage and opened it on the counter beside the phone. If –

The banging of the brightly painted letterbox by the front door alerted her to the arrival of the mail. The box contained the usual assortment of flyers, a couple of bills, and a plain white envelope addressed to M. Saunders. There was no return address.

Back in the kitchen, Mel tossed the flyers and bills aside. She looked at the remaining envelope. It was probably just some marketing letter, selling yet another must-have item, or a pitch for money or donation to a worthy cause of which she had never heard.

Leaning back against the counter, she ripped it open and withdrew the single sheet of neatly folded, white paper. She yawned then shook open the paper to read.

With a furrowed brow and a snicker, she noted the assortment of colorful letters glued to the page. What kind of —

Her amusement was snuffed out as the letters became words and the words a sentence whose menace drove every other thought from her mind.

Leave Key West or your baby dies.

~ ~ ~

. . . your baby dies . . . your baby dies . . . The words swam before Mel's eyes even after the sheet of paper fluttered to the floor from her limp fingers *. . . your baby dies . . .*

She gasped and raced for the bedroom. She yanked the door open and leapt to the side of the crib. Kirsten lay on her back her chubby face turned to one side, sleeping peacefully, her breathing even and sweet.

Mel lowered her head into her hands. Her heart hammered against her chest as hard as a jackhammer on concrete. Kirsten was safe. Thank God she was safe. *For now.*

After a moment, she lowered her hands and gripped the top railing of the crib. She couldn't stop trembling. She stared at the child, but all she saw were those gruesome, mismatched letters spelling out their horrible warning: *Leave Key West or your baby dies.*

What kind of a person would send such a warning? Could it be one of the neighbors, enraged because she hadn't left right away? Or the anonymous crank caller to the child abuse hotline? Was it the same person? The heavy breather perhaps?

With a last look at the sleeping child, she tiptoed out of the room to the kitchen.

She retrieved the paper from the floor and looked at it again, hoping she'd been mistaken, hoping that somehow she'd developed temporary dyslexia and misread the message.

No. The same, horrible, garish letters stared back at her. There was no mistake.

She looked at the phone. Call the police, her head commanded.

Her body refused to obey. She hated talking to cops, answering their questions, seeing the suspicion and scorn on their faces. When she found Kevin, she'd had no choice but to call the police. The result had been that he'd been branded a suicide and a vicious murderer – and she was his sister. The cops didn't care about protecting people like her. They'd barely even looked for Darla's killer. Why would now be any different?

But this was Kirsten. If anything happened to her...

She reached for the phone, then pulled her hand back. She couldn't phone the cops. Not again. She couldn't.

But she had to tell someone. She couldn't take a chance that this was just a crank letter. Not when it came to Kirsten.

In slow motion she went to the kitchen junk drawer and opened it. Right away she saw it, the crumpled card she should have thrown out but had stuffed in the junk drawer instead.

Damien's card. All the numbers for the man who had the least reason to help her, the man who had every reason to hate her.

But he had offered to help. For Kirsten, she would have to take him up on it.

She straightened out the card until she could read his home number, picked up her cell and grudgingly punched Damien in as a New Contact.

Chapter Eighteen

"Why'd you call the police?"

Mel's angry demand caught Damien off guard, even more than the scowl on her face. Calling the police had been his automatic reaction the moment he got off the phone with her. Then he'd thrown on a t-shirt and jeans and raced over.

"Why wouldn't I call the police?" He raised his hands in exasperation. "It's a *death* threat, Mel. Of course I called the police. What did you think I'd do? I called Dan, too."

"Dan? You mean Matthews?" She groaned. "Not him."

"Why not him? He's in homicide, isn't he? Besides, after three deaths of people you know in the last few weeks, it only makes sense."

She became dangerously still, a bad sign. She was shutting him out again. Her voice was quiet and calm, too calm. "Oh. So you still think I had something to do with those murders?"

He grimaced. "That's not what I meant." He moved closer and reached for her.

She flinched away from him and wrapped her arms around her middle. "I knew I should have taken care of this myself. I should never have called you. I don't need your help."

He lifted her chin so she couldn't avoid looking at him. "Maybe you don't need my help. But I *want* to help you. And it's not because I feel sorry for you, or think you aren't capable. I want to help you because I care about you, and about Kirsten, too."

Suspicion flickered in her eyes and he felt her stiffen. He recognized the stubborn set of her jaw.

"Mel, you can't do everything by yourself," he continued. "You've done an amazing job of taking care of Kirsten, and making a good life for her and for Joanie and yourself. Not many people could do as well. But things are crazy now –

each of us has lost a brother and Ryan as well. It's no crime to admit you need help. Or that you want it."

Though her expression didn't change, her eyes glittered with an odd brightness. For a moment, he thought she might acknowledge what he'd just said, admit that he had touched her as she had touched him, that she wanted all the support he could offer, not because she needed it, but because it was from him.

The moment passed. She wrenched away from him. She turned her back, her shoulders tense, arms held tightly at her sides. "I don't need help. I can do this myself. I –"

A sharp rap at the door cut her off.

"Come on in, Dan," Damien said.

Dan had just entered the kitchen when there was a second knock. Two uniformed officers peered around the half-open door. "Is there a Melissa Saunders here?"

"Yes." Mel, Damien and Dan all spoke at once. Mel glared at the two men, then turned back to the uniformed officers. They introduced themselves and she invited them to sit at the two seats at the kitchen table. Dan identified himself. "This lady's been witness to a couple of murders and a suspicious death in the last few weeks. I want to hear the details of this threat."

Damien leaned against the counter and listened while Mel produced the letter and the envelope and explained when and how it arrived.

"Can we take this?" the younger of the two men asked. Mel nodded and with gloved fingers he slipped the envelope and folded paper into an evidence bag.

"Any idea who might have sent this?"

Mel frowned. "Yes, it's –"

A half-hearted cry from the bedroom interrupted her. She stood up. "Excuse me. I have to get Kirsten."

"Can't Joanie take care of her?" Damien asked.

"She's not here."

"Where is she?"

Mel didn't look at him. "She's left. I got up today and found a note saying she's moving out and would be back in a couple of days to get the rest of her things."

"Have you still got that note?"

White-faced, Mel went to the cabinet under the sink and pulled out the recycle bin. The lid sprang up, and with two fingers she extracted a crumpled strip of paper, one end of which was damp.

"Pickle juice." She wiped it off with a paper towel.

Kirsten's cries escalated to screams. Mel dropped the paper on the table and bolted for the bedroom.

Dan read the note, then slipped it into another bag. He looked up at Damien. "Think the roommate might be behind the death threat? She took Kevin Saunders' death pretty hard. She was pretty steamed at his funeral. Seemed to think it was all his sister's fault."

Damien frowned. "Don't know." He noticed the stack of tattered magazines on the coffee table. "Maybe you should check those magazines over there for missing pages and cutout words."

A couple of minutes later Mel returned to the kitchen. Kirsten in her arms, she went straight to the refrigerator and brought out a bottle of baby formula. While the child squirmed about to gawk at the four men, Mel took off the lid, put the open bottle in the microwave and reheated it. To the delight of the men, including Damien, Kirsten smiled at each of them, cooing and drooling onto her shoulder.

"How could anyone threaten this little charmer?" the second of the two policemen asked. "Reminds me of my own daughter at home."

Mel settled Kirsten in her high chair. The child took the warmed bottle and started sucking ravenously.

"You were about to tell us who could have sent the threatening letter to you," the first officer prompted.

Mel made a face. "I guess it could be any one of the neighbors. They circulated a petition to get us evicted. Mr. Rubenstein – he's the landlord living in the front cottage with his wife – brought it over yesterday."

Damien pressed his lips together. *Why hadn't she told him that before?* It certainly explained her over-reaction to the presence of the temp security guard at Viva Zapata last evening.

"Where's the petition?" he demanded. "Did you agree to leave?"

"Mr. Rubenstein's got it." She paused and looked from Dan to Damien. "And I did say we'd leave, but not until I find a new place. I told him it would probably take a while."

"Maybe that wasn't fast enough for your neighbors," Damien said darkly.

Dan gave him a warning look. "Is there anyone else who might have sent the letter?"

Kirsten started to choke. Mel took the bottle, picked the child up, and started patting her back.

Damien stepped forward. "I'll take her. You concentrate on the questions."

To his surprise, she relinquished the baby. He took the bottle, and leaned back against the counter. Drooling, Kirsten reached for the bottle. He smiled, and she settled happily into his arms.

Mel looked at the floor. "Well, there was the mouth breather."

"The what?"

"A couple of weeks ago. Around the time that Tony Flores was killed. Joanie and I kept getting these heavy breather calls on our landline. Whoever it was never said anything, just did the breathing thing then hung up. I changed to an unlisted number and the calls stopped."

"What about the anonymous complaint to the child-abuse hotline?" Damien prompted from his position at the counter. "That was shortly after Ryan's death."

She flushed. "Yeah, that too."

"Care to explain, Ms. Saunders?"

She continued to look at the floor. "Someone phoned the hotline to say –"

There was a rap on the now opened screen door. An officious-looking middle-aged black woman with graying hair stepped into the kitchen. She stopped short when she saw the police officers and the other men congregating in the small room.

Damien glanced at Mel, who clearly recognized the woman.

"I'm from the Department of Children and Families," the woman said. "I need to speak to Ms. Saunders, in private. There's been another complaint to the child abuse hotline."

~ ~ ~

Kirsten responded to Betty Leeson's loving embrace the way every child had always responded to Mel's foster parent. She gurgled happily and settled deeper into the woman's experienced arms.

"See? She'll be fine." From her place on the sofa in the sunroom at the back of the tiny Conch cottage, Betty looked up at Mel. "You don't have to worry about her."

"Good." With relief Mel put down the diaper bag stuffed with disposables and bottles of formula, some jars of baby food and the backpack of clothes. She'd been on the edge of falling apart all afternoon, and the arrival of the police and then the investigator from Children and Families Services had only made things worse. Thank God the social worker knew Betty and Don Leeson. Both she and the police had agreed bringing Kirsten here for a few days was a good idea.

Mel straightened. "Damien is bringing more formula and baby food."

Over her reading glasses, Betty regarded her kindly. With her short blue-gray curls and plump figure, Betty looked like everyone's favorite grandmother. But behind those floral dresses and steel-rimmed glasses was a strong woman who missed little and didn't mince words. "Your young man seems very nice," she said quietly.

"He's not my young man," Mel corrected. "He's my boss. About-to-be former boss for that matter."

"That's all?" Betty raised one powdered eyebrow. "If he's not your young man, looks to me as if he'd sure like to be."

Tension knotted Mel's stomach again. Betty meant well, but . . .

"It's not like that," she said as evenly as she could. "I told you about Kevin's suicide. But it's worse than that. The police think Kevin killed Damien's brother too, as well as Ryan from the club."

For a moment Betty said nothing. She rocked Kirsten back and forth, then looked up at Mel again. "And you think he blames you for the murders?"

"No," she had to admit. At least for the moment, Damien didn't blame her. "But it doesn't matter. Even if it's okay with him now, even if he's okay with it, it's not okay with me. It won't ever be okay with me."

"Hmm." Betty's gaze commanded Mel's attention. "Tell me, could you have prevented the murders? If, indeed, Kevin committed those murders, could you have stopped him?"

Mel frowned. "I don't see how."

"And so, if the brother you hardly knew killed two men, you're going to hold yourself responsible for the rest of your life? Is that it?"

Mel dropped her chin down. She didn't know how to answer that.

"If there's one thing my years as a foster parent have taught me, as well as my forty-seven years of marriage, it's that you should never underestimate the human heart. It has an unlimited capacity to love and, perhaps more importantly, to forgive."

"Yeah, well . . . ." Mel felt like the skinny eleven-year-old again, hanging her head and rubbing her foot in the dirt, refusing to look at her new foster mother because she might discover just how scared she really was.

Betty juggled Kirsten into one arm and patted the slipcovered sofa. Reluctantly Mel sat down beside her.

Shaking her head, Betty put her arm around Mel and hugged her. "Ah, my sweet girl."

She squeezed her shoulder and talked, repeating a scenario that had taken place many times in the last fourteen years. "You were always so fierce, even in the beginning. You wouldn't let anyone get near you, wouldn't divulge any of your secrets or inner thoughts. You never cried, not one drop. I remember that first year; you were even suspicious of your Christmas presents. I swear, you thought we were going to take them away from you as soon as you opened them. It took us a good half hour to convince you they were yours to keep."

The hand on her arm stilled. "I thought you'd begun to trust, at least a little. But maybe I was wrong." She paused and looked hard at Mel. "You know, it's not weakness to accept help. Especially now. You've been through so much. A weaker person would have broken long ago."

Betty lightly kissed Mel's cheek. "Cut yourself some slack, sweetie. Let that young man of yours help you. Lord knows he wants to."

"Well, here we are."

With a patently fake groan, Don Leeson staggered into the room, a box of baby food in his skinny arms. He tossed his head to throw back the strands of longish gray hair hanging in his leathery face. "You plan to leave this child here for a year?" he boomed.

Behind him stood Damien, another box of food in his arms. His expression was carefully neutral, but his dark gaze roamed the room in curiosity, finally lighting on Mel. He smiled then, and for a second she forgot about everyone else.

"Oh, quit complaining, Don. This is the first real work you've done in weeks. Besides, you love Kirsten." Betty turned to Mel. "You can leave her here as long as necessary. It'll give us a chance to get to know her better."

Mel took Kirsten, hugged her, and handed her back to Betty. She stood up. "I don't know how long it will be. I hope just a few days."

Damien put down his box and shook hands with Don. As Don and Mel headed for the door, Damien nodded a good bye to Betty and turned to leave.

"Just a moment, young man. I'd like to have a word with you."

Mel winced and turned back but Don grabbed her arm. "You know better than to mess with Betty when she's got somethin' to say. Come on, out to the car with you." Smiling, he urged her down the long hallway leaving an unsuspecting Damien behind.

Mel sighed. She had a pretty good idea what Betty was going to say to Damien.

Outside, Don guided her to Damien's Infiniti, opened the door with a flourish, and then shut it after her. Grinning, he leaned in the window. "Chin up, Mellie. I know this is rough for you, but we'll take good care of Kirsten. Never you fear."

The front door of the shotgun house slammed and Damien came out. Mel watched him. He looked serious and determined as he strode to the car.

Don whistled. "Looks like he's got his marching orders." He tousled Mel's unadorned hair. "Be good, kid. We'll see you in a couple of days." He stepped back, made a mock salute and headed back to the house.

Damien got in and started the car. For the first time that day, Mel noticed the dark stubble on his jaw and cheeks. His uncombed hair stuck up in a couple of places, his t-shirt was rumpled, and one knee of his jeans was ripped and grass-stained.

Her throat tightened. At her call, he had jumped out of bed, thrown on the first clothes handy and raced to her cottage. He hadn't showered, he hadn't eaten – he probably still hadn't eaten and it was after five.

And he'd done it all without complaint, without question. For her. Her throat filled and she bit her lip. Could Betty be right?

Damien drove for several minutes before speaking. "Don't you want to know what Betty said to me?"

Mel shook her head. "I already know. Something along the lines of, *"You're dead meat if anything happens to Mel."*

He laughed. "Well, not quite as blunt as that, but pretty close." He paused, then glanced at her. "So where are we going?"

"Home."

"Mel." His voice held a warning note. "You know –"

"I need to get dressed for work. And pick up some clothes and toiletries to take to your house."

Blood Ties in Key West

"Oh." He sounded surprised. "That was easy."

She turned and smiled at him. "Betty's good. I might be stubborn but I'm not stupid. I know when I'm beat."

~ ~ ~

In the flashing lights from the dance floor, Damien watched Mel weave her way through the standing room only people around the bar. As usual, a headset framed her face, and she stopped to talk to anyone stepping out of line. She looked slim and beautiful in her standard black, but something was missing.

With a start, he realized what it was. The swagger that characterized her walk to the pounding beat of the music, the arrogant assurance she wore like a suit of armor, it was gone. Tonight's Mel was quiet, pale, subdued, definitely not herself. He'd suggested she not come to work tonight, that she rest at his place instead. But when she'd insisted, he'd been relieved. He wasn't sure why; he just felt better having her in his sights.

He frowned. What kind of a psycho would threaten a baby? For any resident of that quiet street to have done it seemed extreme, but it was the logical place to start. That, and the anonymous caller to Mel's landline and the abuse hotline. He continued to watch Mel, amazed at the tensions she'd faced over the past few weeks, and faced alone. It was a wonder she hadn't crumbled, or worse, cut and run.

"Hola!" From the doorway, Alonzo Salva hailed Damien. He pointed to his office and headed back inside. A moment later his lawyer joined him. He wore cargo shorts and a short-sleeved shirt, a signal that he'd been home before coming here, but carried a wide lawyer's briefcase.

Alonzo nodded at the door. "What's with your bouncer? Looks like she's lost most of her bounce."

"Yeah." So it wasn't evident only to Damien. Quickly he filled Alonzo in on the day's events, and what had happened in the previous week. "She's staying with me for a few days until the police get a handle on who sent the threat and how serious it is."

Susan Haskell

Alonzo put down his briefcase and screwed up his face. "Is that wise, Damien? So far, it looks as if her brother killed Tony and Ryan, and likely tried to kill you too. It's bad enough that she's still working here for even a couple more days. But to take her into your home?"

"Mel isn't her brother," Damien said flatly. Alonzo didn't need to know his doubts about whether Kevin was the killer. "She's a decent person trying her best to raise her niece. I'm not going to blame her for being his sister."

"But your home? Isn't that going a bit far? You've got to know this isn't making negotiations with Cristina over the business any easier. Once she hears what you've done, she'll have a fit. She'll never settle for anything reasonable."

Widow or not, Damien was fed up with Cristina and her histrionics. "It's none of Cristina's business. In fact, there's no reason for her to know at all, unless *you* tell her. Or Maduro puts a tail on me."

"I wouldn't put it past him," Alonzo muttered. He picked up his briefcase, set it on Damien's desk and snapped it open. "What's this about you sneaking into his garage to look at his bike?"

"Is that what he told you?" Damien snorted. "I don't give a damn about his bike. It was Tony's Zuma I was looking for, and no thanks to Esteban, it wasn't even there. The guy didn't have a clue it had been stolen."

"Stolen?" Alonzo withdrew several legal-sized papers from his briefcase. He straightened and looked at Damien. "You don't think that could have been the bike Saunders used when he shot at you?"

"Until we find Tony's scooter, there's no way of knowing." Damien turned to the matter at hand. "You've got the amended copies of the will?"

"Yes. We've made all the changes you wanted. All you have to do now is sign."

Damien sat down behind his desk and took the papers. He skimmed over the clauses he'd already read thoroughly the other day, then grabbed a pen and scrawled his name at the place where Alonzo's secretary Marla had marked an 'x'."

He flipped to the second copy and added his signature there. While his mother was alive and owned the business, he'd never bothered with a will. But now that he was the only Flores left, Alonzo had been insistent that he have a will. For the time being, almost everything had been left to Cristina, with a small portion of the businesses going to his cousin, Enrique, who had worked summers in one of the Latin Lovers stores during high school and college. The details would likely change once he and Cristina reached an agreement concerning her share of the business, but until then, this will was a necessary precaution.

Pen still poised over the will, he looked up at Alonzo. "Want me to call Gord in to witness?"

Alonzo shook his head. "Marla can do it in the morning."

"Fine." Damien put the copies together and was about to hand them back to Alonzo when his gaze fell on the clause leaving a portion of the businesses and house to his cousin Enrique. *Or at least the clause where that should have been.*

He looked at it more closely. "There's something wrong here. Where's the clause about Enrique?"

"Give me that!" Alonzo grabbed the document out of Damien's hands. He looked at it. His neck reddened. "Oh, that *come pinga*! She can be such a ditz!" He muttered something about how his secretary must have inadvertently left the clause out when she made the amendments on the computer that morning.

Damien knew he meant Marla. He'd met her before, and it wasn't the first time she'd screwed up, though in all honesty, Alonzo should have caught it.

Alonzo stuffed the papers into his briefcase. "I'll come by tomorrow night with the amended copies, all right?"

A loud crash that sounded as if it was near the bar distracted Damien. "Sure," he said, jumping up and heading for the door. "Anytime after seven."

~ ~ ~

It was no good. Damien had been lying in bed staring at the ceiling of his room for more than an hour and he was still wide-awake. Still aching for the woman who was probably sound asleep by now in the room next to his.

But no, he had to be the gentleman. Knowing how tired Mel was, knowing how hard today had been for her – knowing the last place she wanted to be was here, in his home – he had shown her to his old room, the one his mother had redecorated in turquoise and terracotta after he left home for the first time.

Now, no matter what his head said, the rest of him knew a beautiful, desirable woman was in the next room. A woman who had made love with him before, a woman who had given him a taste of all that could be between them. A woman who wanted him, and would want him again – perhaps even love him – if he could only get beyond her defenses.

A bedspring protested nearby and he was instantly alert. Hope sprang anew. He flung back the covers, pulled on a pair of athletic shorts hanging on the arm of the chair, and started for the hallway.

If there was any chance Mel had changed her mind, he didn't intend to miss it.

~ ~ ~

It was no good. No matter how she tried, Mel couldn't go to sleep. Maybe it was the strange bed in a strange room in a strange house. Maybe she missed the comforting sound of Kirsten's even breaths, the reassuring rustles every now and then from the nearby crib.

Or maybe it was knowing that the man who had helped her despite all the naysayers, the gentleman who had taken her into his home without expectation of reward, was in the next room, in bed, alone. Alone and, she hoped, wanting her. Yearning for her as she couldn't help yearning for him.

She rolled to her side and stared at the wall. Alone. She was used to being alone. Usually she liked it. But now it was different. She felt lonely, empty, restless. She wanted to see the gleam in Damien's rich brown eyes, inhale his musky scent, feel his hands and lips on every part of her. But most of all she just wanted to be with him.

In frustration she squirmed about, kicking the blankets off. Was Betty right? Should she trust Damien? Should she stop pushing him away? Should she – *could* she – believe that the kindness and affection she'd seen in Damien's eyes and in his actions were genuine? And that what members of their respective families had done or not done didn't matter?

She sighed. On more than one occasion he had taken the first step, including today, when he had teamed up with Betty to convince her to come here. Was it up to her to take the next step?

The groan of bedsprings somewhere nearby galvanized her into action. She sat up, swung her feet to the floor, pulled down her nightshirt, and headed for the door. She didn't want a gentleman. Not when Damien was next door.

Barefoot she padded through the half-open doorway into the hallway beyond. It was even darker than in her room. Her hand on the wall, she took a couple of steps to the left towards Damien's room.

Without warning she collided with a hard, warm body. "Oof!"

"Mel?"

"Damien?"

Her hands slid unerringly up his chest to his neck at the same moment he cupped her bottom and gathered her close. His lips found hers and she welcomed him with a murmur of joy.

The kiss deepened and grew and before she realized it, her back was against the wall, her legs around his narrow hips and she was kissing and moving against him and it still wasn't enough. From some far away place she heard whimpers and small sounds of pleasures and recognized only vaguely that it was her voicing her desire.

She dragged her lips along the rough stubble of Damien's jaw, then tasted the salty sheen of sweat on his throat. She bit his shoulder. "Now, Damien," she whispered raggedly. "I'm all yours."

Chapter Nineteen

Damien's answer was to grasp her hip and scoop her into his arms. He kicked open his bedroom door and carried her inside. A bedside lamp illuminated a king-size expanse of bed, the covers thrown back. Gently he deposited her amidst the pillows and crumpled sheets. He started to step back but she pulled him down to the bed until their lips joined once more and his body covered hers.

After a heated moment, he dragged his lips away. He grinned, a wicked gleam in his dark eyes. "If I'd known you were this anxious for me, I'd never have put you in the room next door."

She tried unsuccessfully to reclaim his lips. "If I'd know you were such a gentleman – and such a tease – I'd never have come here."

He cocked an eyebrow. His thumbs caressed the wrists he held loosely over her head. He kissed her forehead, and feathered kisses along her cheek to her chin. "A tease, huh? And all this time I thought you were pushing me way."

A lump formed in her throat. "I - I never wanted to push you away."

His eyes darkened to the deep, unending black of the night. "I know," he said, and somehow she knew that he did. His lips curved upward in that smile, together with his kindness and generosity, that had found its way to her most secret places, warming and reviving the faith and trust that had all but withered away.

"It doesn't matter now," he said, nuzzling her cheek. "Because now I'm going to love you like you've never been loved before." His smile widened. "By the time I'm through, you'll have decided to take up residence in this bed permanently."

"Yeah?" she challenged, blinking hard against the unaccustomed sting of tears. He was teasing, but beneath it was an affection that breached all the barriers she'd erected. She tried to salvage her bravado. "And you think you're man enough to do that?"

"We'll find out, won't we?"

He leaned forward on his knees, pulled the cotton tee up over her arms and head and tossed it behind him. He gathered her aching breasts in his warm hands, stroking the budding nipples with his thumbs. He lowered his head, at the last second looking up at her. "You sure about this?"

His mouth closed over one nipple and she inhaled sharply.

"Yes, Damien, yes!"

~ ~ ~

Morning light streamed through an opening between the curtains when Mel finally snuggled back into Damien's arms. She pulled his hand around her waist and wriggled her bare bottom until she was firmly nestled up against him. She sighed in contentment. "Who'd ever have thought Damien Flores was a marathon lover?"

He nibbled on her ear lobe. "Mi amor, that's only the first of the many secrets you're going to learn about me."

Mel liked the sound of that. Maybe this trusting someone wasn't such a bad idea. Especially when it was Damien.

She lifted his hand, and kissed the tip of each long finger. "Why are you so good to me?"

"How could I be anything else?" He kissed the tender spot behind her ear. "You know I'm falling in love with you."

Falling in love with you? The words that had always terrified her more than the biggest bruiser in a bar didn't seem quite so scary now. That didn't mean she knew how to respond to them.

"Go to sleep, Damien," she murmured pulling his arm more tightly around her waist.

She closed her eyes and tried to pretend nothing had changed. No matter what happened when they woke up, she knew she would never forget what he'd just said, and all that had gone on before.

She hoped he wouldn't forget either.

Blood Ties in Key West

~ ~ ~

It was after two p.m. when Damien woke up. Mel still spooned into his body. Careful not to wake her, he extricated one arm, then the other, and slid off the far side of the bed. In moments he had donned clean jeans and t-shirt and slipped his feet into his boat shoes sticking out haphazardly from under the bed.

Longingly, he looked back at his bed where Mel still slept. She looked good there, her hair wild and dark against the pale blue sheets, one arm flung over her eyes. He hoped he'd be able to keep her, not just in his bed, but also in every part of his life.

For now, there was something he had to do. The idea had started gnawing at him yesterday, in Mel's kitchen, when she and the police talked about who might have sent the threatening letter. He'd thought about it on and off at work, but it hadn't really hit him until Alonzo had brought in the will for him to sign. Even then, he hadn't wanted to believe it could be true. Could it be Cristina?

But who else hated Mel beyond reason, beyond common sense? Even knowing all the facts, Cristina persisted in believing that Mel had purposely thrown Tony outside to be killed. The fact that Kevin Saunders was the likely killer only increased her hatred and hardened her belief that Mel had been in on it. She'd likely seen Damien's relationship with Mel as the final betrayal.

It was a long shot, but one Damien wanted to put to rest before he negotiated any settlement of the business. Cristina was no killer, of that he had no doubt. But a campaign of anonymous calls and letters? Maybe. Even in Tony's memory, he'd be damned if he'd give a cent to her if she was behind this drive to get Mel out of Key West.

He picked up a pad from the dresser and scrawled a short note. He didn't want Mel to think he'd abandoned her, especially not in his own bed. He placed the note beside her on the sheet and took one last, lingering look.

Susan Haskell

She was so beautiful. He'd never met anyone like her. Rough and tough, yes, but a big heart, and kind and responsible, too.

He grinned. Had he mentioned hot? The memories of their lovemaking sizzled through him as he headed for the door. He wanted to get this over with quick, and get back in time for more before they both had to go to work.

Fifteen minutes later he arrived at the Key West by the Sea condos. He always managed to miss the entrance so entered using the exit, resulting in driving through the parking lot from the wrong direction. He hoped he would not be scolded by a resident as he had in the past.

The pale coral five-story buildings on acres of lush tropic foliage overlooked Smathers Beach, the largest beach on the island. Damien had always loved the view of the azure Atlantic. He headed to the gate by the clubhouse. It had been a long time since he had used the key Tony had given to him to swim laps whenever he wanted to. Today he would use it to enter the property to pay a visit to Cristina. He was counting on the element of surprise to help him find the truth.

The hallway outside her condo was deserted. Damien knocked on the door, then stood out of range of the peephole. He heard a woman's voice, and then the door swung open.

A yellow bulge of a maternity blouse was the first thing Damien saw. Eyes wide with surprise, he looked up.

He recognized her face at the exact instant she recognized him. Shock, then horror, twisted her features. For a second, she didn't move. Then she grabbed for the door and tried to slam it shut.

Chapter Twenty

Mel rolled over and reached for Damien. Groggily she opened one eye, then the other, while her hand searched the sheets. She sat up. "Damien?"

A small square of paper lay on the bed beside her, words scrawled across it. She picked it up. "Be back soon," Damien had scrawled. "Don't leave." The "don't" was underlined, and followed by the words "I love you" and his initials D.E.F.

I love you. Holding the note tightly, she shut her eyes. So she hadn't imagined he said he was falling in love with her. She opened her eyes. Because there it was, in writing, right in front of her. And it didn't seem anywhere near as terrifying as it had in the early hours of this morning.

No, it was wonderful. And as solid, and real and believable and absolutely amazing as the man himself. Damien loved her!

Giddily, she stared at the note. She wanted to kiss it, to throw it in the air, to open the windows and shout that Damien loved her. She smiled so widely her jaw hurt. Which wasn't like her at all. All that loving must have gone to her head.

She pushed back the sheets and swung her feet to the floor. Her eyes gazed unhurriedly around the master bedroom of the Classical Revival 'eyebrow' house. She had heard of this uniquely Key West architectural design but had never been inside one. She could see the roof extending down over the second-story windows onto white porch columns which compromised the view but did wonders for shading the second floor. The bedroom was immense, the dark oiled teak furniture unabashedly masculine in a streamlined, modern style. Mel suspected Damien had replaced his parents' furniture, at least in this room, after his mother died.

Susan Haskell

She found her t-shirt on the floor, pulled it over her head, and padded out to the hall. At the door to her room, she paused. "Damien?" she called. Her voice echoed unanswered through the empty house.

In the guest room where she'd started out, her black backpack sat on a straight-back mahogany chair in the corner by the window. After a last look at the note, she carefully slid it into a side pocket. No matter what happened now, she would always have this note.

She took the backpack and headed back to Damien's room. He'd shown her a bathroom down the hall, but she wanted to use the master ensuite. Showering in his shower, with his soap, surrounded by his towels and toiletries, made it all seem more real, and him closer than ever. Silly maybe, but for once, she'd like to indulge herself.

Hot water rained down upon her and she sang in the steam and the heat. She soaped herself with his soap, inhaling the scent she recognized from Damien's skin and hair. She dried herself with his still-damp towel, imagining his touch and his kisses embracing her body as intimately as the towel. She grinned at herself in the steamed-up mirror. *Was this how it felt to love someone who loved you back?*

Quickly she dressed in her usual black spandex trousers and a sleeveless black top. She would have preferred to wear something else, something bright and happy that reflected her mood, but she'd only brought work clothes. And the truth of the matter was, she didn't own anything bright, just a closet-full of dark, sober clothing.

By the time she went downstairs to the large, open kitchen, it was already three-thirty. Using the house phone on the bead board wall, she called Betty.

"Kirsten is great," Betty informed her. "She's just up from her nap and Don has her out for a walk. It's been so long since we've had a baby in the house, we'd forgotten how much fun it is."

"And how much work, too," added Mel. Guiltily she remembered what she *should* be doing right now: Trying to find Joanie, and if that failed, finding another babysitter. "I'll be over around four tomorrow to see Kirsten," she promised.

"Give my best to your young man," Betty said.

Mel didn't bother correcting her. Maybe Damien was going to be her 'man' after all, a possibility she'd never allowed herself to entertain about anyone before.

After saying her goodbyes, she opened the refrigerator and a couple of cupboards, searching for something to eat. Damien had a surprisingly well-stocked fridge, probably a result of owning the cantina business. But most of the fresh stuff was untouched and past its 'best before' date.

She poured herself a tall glass of orange juice and sat at the kitchen table looking out the French doors to the gorgeous backyard. Just beyond the wraparound deck with its painted blue ceiling, was a sparkling cocktail pool with a rock waterfall and massive-leafed plants and fruit trees making the backyard look like a tropical oasis.

She finished the juice and went back to the cupboard. Maybe just some cereal for now. As she reached for the granola, she heard a bang. It sounded as if something had fallen on the floor.

She walked from the kitchen to the dining room that led to the living room, but she didn't think the noise had come from that direction. She stood and listened. Nothing.

Returning to the kitchen, she looked down the main hallway. She hadn't toured the house last night, but she could see at least two doors off the hallway, most likely a powder room and library or den.

She stood and listened. Still nothing. It wasn't her house, and she was reluctant to snoop into areas where she hadn't been invited. But if there was something wrong . . .

She turned back to the granola, when she heard something else. A faint clanging and squeak, like a drawer in a metal filing cabinet being closed. She went to the hallway again. Could Damien have come back?

"Damien?"

When there was no answer, she crept towards the first door. It was slightly ajar.

Susan Haskell

She opened it. A dark-haired man in a faded t-shirt and jeans stood by the far wall, in front of a bank of wooden filing cabinets, his back to her. His build and hair color were similar to Damien's.

"Damien?"

The man whirled around to face her.

She blinked in shock. "You? What are you doing here?"

~ ~ ~

Damien jammed his foot between the frame and the swiftly shutting door. He grabbed the door and pried it open, then shouldered his way inside.

Joanie stepped back, her eyes huge, her hands clenched at her sides.

Damien straightened. "This is a surprise. What are you doing here?"

The girl stuck out her lower lip. "I live here now. Cristina wanted a roommate."

"A roommate, huh?" Damien snorted. "Maybe Cristina should have called Mel first and asked her about how *reliable* you are . . . or if you paid any rent."

Joanie flushed but maintained her belligerent stance. "I don't have to –"

"Stop badgering her, Damien." Cristina entered the living room from the hallway. The white capris and camisole she wore, along with the white-blonde hair piled on her head, made her look as cool as she sounded. "Who lives here now is no one's business but mine."

"Maybe. But if you're expecting her to help you with the rent, you're barking up the wrong tree."

"Get out. I don't know why you're here anyway, especially after our last conversation. Leave, NOW."

"No," Damien said calmly. "I need a few answers from you."

Cristina stalked over to a table in the entranceway. With her back to Damien, she opened a drawer. When she whirled around, her expression triumphant, she held a Smith and Wesson .38 trained right at him. "You aren't getting anything from me. Get out."

Damien's gut tightened, but his expression didn't change. "Why'd you get a gun, Cristina? Planning on hurting someone?"

"It's for protection," she snapped. "Esteban got it for me, for moments just like this. Now get out."

He shook his head. "Nope. Not until you tell me why you hate Mel so much."

Cristina looked at him as if he were stupid. "You know why. She threw Tony out of the club to be killed. She probably gave him the drugs that made him get violent. And even if she didn't, her brother killed Tony. Isn't that enough?"

Damien jerked his head in Joanie's direction. "Given what you just said, it surprises me that you'd want Joanie here."

Cristina frowned. She lowered the gun slightly. "Why should that make a difference? Joanie hates Mel as much as I do."

Joanie started to sidle along the couch towards the hallway. She put her hand on her belly. "I'm not feeling very well. I think I'll –"

"Tell her whose baby you're carrying, Joanie."

The girl blanched. "It's – it's none of her business."

Damien continued, his voice hard. "If you don't tell her, I will."

"Don't believe anything he says, Cristina." Joanie's voice cracked on the last few words.

Cristina waved the gun at Damien. "I've had enough of your pathetic attempts to rattle me. Get out."

"It's Kevin Saunders' baby," Damien said flatly. "That's why Kevin was found dead outside their apartment door. He had just left after visiting Joanie – the mother of his child."

"What?" Cristina's voice rose to a screech. She turned on Joanie, the gun hanging at her side. "You said you hated Mel as much as I did. But you . . . you . . ."

Her words sputtered out. Her shoulders shook with rage. She raised the pistol and pointed it at the girl now cowering against the couch. "How could you –?"

Susan Haskell

Damien leapt across the room and grabbed Cristina's wrist just as she pulled the trigger.

~ ~ ~

Neither the smile beneath the dark mustache nor the reassurance in the soulful eyes convinced Mel that Alonzo Salva was up to any good. He faced her, his right hand in the cabinet's open drawer.

"What are you doing here?" She repeated. "I didn't hear the doorbell."

"That's because I have a key," he said pleasantly. "When I didn't see Damien's car, I thought no one was here."

"Yeah?" A lifetime of being fed lies and false assurances by people she knew or was related to had made Mel distrustful of everyone. Even for Damien's lawyer, it was difficult to set aside her suspicions.

Alonzo laughed and gestured with his free hand. "If you look around, you'll see this is Damien's home office. I'm in and out of it all the time."

A quick glance told her that he was right. But still . . . If he was working, why wasn't he wearing a suit? Didn't lawyers always wear suits to work?

"I might ask what *you're* doing here?" he continued.

She glared at him. After seeing him so often in the company of Cristina, who hated her guts, she wasn't about to tell him anything. "It's none of your business," she snapped and turned to leave.

"Ah, but it is."

The odd comment made her pause and glance back. "What?"

The placid expression on his face had disappeared, replaced by a look so venomous and full of hatred that she froze.

"What do –?"

Then she saw it. He had pulled his hand from the drawer and with it, a revolver.

He pointed it at her. "Did you really think a dumb-ass broad like you was going to get all of Damien's money?"

He clicked the safety off and sneered. "If you did, you're as stupid as your brother is."

The sneer turned into a nasty smile. "Or was."

Chapter Twenty-One

The gun discharged just as Damien yanked Cristina's arm down towards the floor. It flew out of her hand, and skidded across the saltillo tile floor to the mirrored wall.

Damien grabbed her other arm and dragged her down to the sofa. "What's wrong with you?" he hissed. "Are you trying to end up in jail – or dead?"

"Get the gun, Joanie! Get the gun and shoot him!" Cristina screeched.

Joanie cowered against the wall, her arms folded protectively over her belly. Her terrified gaze flitted from Cristina to the gun on the floor, then back again. She didn't move.

Damien shook Cristina. "*Idiota estupida*! Quit acting like an idiot. You're in enough trouble already without counseling Joanie to shoot me."

At the mention of her name again, Joanie edged farther along the wall and out of range of Cristina. "She did it, you know."

"*Callate!*" screamed Cristina.

"Don't tell her to shut up Cristina." He turned back to Joanie.

"Did what Joanie?" asked Damien.

"Left that threatening letter for Mel. She's the one who phoned the child abuse hotline, too. And made those heavy breather calls."

Damien's eyes narrowed. "So what are *you* doing here?"

Joanie flushed. "I was mad at Mel. Especially after Kevin was killed. Even before that. Mel kept telling me not to go back to Kevin, that he was no good."

She looked at Damien, her gaze wistful. "Mel was right. Kevin abandoned me right after he found out I was pregnant. That's when I came and lived with her. But when he came back, I wanted to believe he had changed. That things would be different. Mel wouldn't listen."

When she was through, Damien nodded at the phone. "Call Detective Matthews." He rattled off the number. Steering a wide berth around the sofa and Cristina, Joanie headed for the phone.

"Don't do it!" Cristina wailed. "Damien forced his way in. We can have him charged. We can –"

"It's too late for that," interrupted Damien. Joanie picked up the receiver and punched in the number. "Besides, after hearing what you did to Mel, Detective Matthews is probably going to have some new questions for you about Kevin Saunders' death. Tony and Ryan's too."

Cristina's face blanched. Despite her arms pinned behind her back, she twisted to try to face him. "You can't mean that, Damien. You know I loved Tony. I quit my job to take care of him. I'd do anything for him."

Unfortunately, Damien did believe her. But he also believed she had tried to ruin Mel's life, because of her twisted belief that Mel – rather than Tony's own weaknesses – had caused his death. And for that – and her threats to an innocent baby – she deserved to pay.

When Damien said nothing, Cristina's pleading turned to renewed rage. "It's you, isn't it?" she said savagely, struggling against his hold. "You're trying to prevent me from getting what was Tony's." She straightened, twisted and cast him a triumphant look. "Well, fat chance. Alonzo warned me about this."

"Alonzo? What does Alonzo have to do with this?"

She sniffed. "He may be your lawyer, Damien, but he's *my* friend – and Tony's. He loves me too. He said he'd make sure I got what should have been Tony's."

She raised her chin. "And more."

The truth hit Damien right hard. *Alonzo and Cristina?* How could he have not seen it before?

Alonzo Salva was the lover Cristina had taken while Tony was in rehab.

~ ~ ~

"You'll never . . . get away . . . with this," gasped Mel.

With the rough rope of the noose taut against her throat and her hands cuffed behind her back, she teetered on a tiny bench in the office, only a toehold between herself and death by hanging from the high exposed beams.

"Of course, I will." Alonzo smiled pleasantly. He sat on a chair just out of reach of a kick from her. "You don't get to be a lawyer by being stupid."

He paused. "Unlike, for example, a former cop who inherits all his mama and papa's wealth."

His eyes met hers. "And unlike a bouncer. Or her brain-dead brother."

"You . . . you killed my brother?"

"That's right. That was the plan all along. The Flores brothers would die, and the no-good ex-con drug dealer would take the blame."

Alonzo's lip curled. "Unfortunately, your brother was a screw-up from the start. He got the coke and stole the Zuma from Maduro's garage, but refused to do the killing. He even messed up on turning out the lights at the club when I tried to stab Damien. But in the end, it all worked out. He was still the patsy and I --"

"You . . . killed . . . Kevin?" Mel choked out. "Just the way you killed Tony and Ryan."

Alonzo smiled. "And the way I'll kill you. And Damien, too. No, it will all work out in my favor. *Finalmente.*"

Mel wobbled on her straining toes, and the rope tightened in warning before she righted herself. She had to do something before it was too late. To her surprise, Alonzo had managed to anticipate every move she'd made, preventing her from either disarming him or escaping. And now she was in the position she'd always sworn to avoid – *victim.*

"I'll . . . write that suicide note now. I promise," she gasped. The gun shoved in her back, she'd already refused to write the note he demanded, a note confessing to Damien's murder and to her own suicide. But now it might buy her another chance.

He shook his head. "Forget it. I've already thought of something else. Once you're both dead, a note won't be necessary. The final scene will speak for itself."

Mel shuddered. Her toes and calves ached from straining to stay upright. But she couldn't stop trying.

"Damien's not . . . stupid. Once . . . once he gets here . . . he'll know something's wrong . . . He'll call the police."

"Macho man?" Alonzo sneered. "No way. He may not be as spoiled and weak as Tony, but he's used to everything going his way. Money, jobs, women – it's always been that way. He won't suspect anything's wrong."

He leaned back into the chair, and stroked the gun with his latex-covered hand. "Besides, I'm looking forward to seeing him suffer. To know all that he's losing – and I'm gaining – before he dies."

The rev of a car engine sounded nearby, and then the slam of a car door. Alonzo sat up straight and adjusted his grip on the pistol. Damien's pistol.

Mel's throat constricted. She pressed her lips together. *Oh, don't let it be Damien, please God,* she prayed.

The front door opened, "Mel?"

Her heart sank. It was Damien.

"Where are you?"

Alonzo shot Mel a triumphant look, then stood and took a position behind the door to the office.

~ ~ ~

Damien looked around the kitchen. Drawers had been yanked open and their contents strewn on the floor amidst shattered glasses and dishes. "Mel?" he called.

There was no answer. He started for the stairs to the second floor, then veered off to his office when he saw the locked filing cabinet drawer hanging open. He suspected the service revolver he kept in one of them would be gone. Could Alonzo have gotten here before Dan sent the officers to pick him up?

He stopped and listened. Who was there?

He was about to check the upstairs bedroom where he had left Mel when he heard a noise. Was that a cough? And where was it coming from? Could it possibly be Mel?

Quietly he retraced his steps. He stood in the middle of the kitchen and listened. He pulled a carving knife from the nearest drawer. It wasn't as good as a gun, but it was better than nothing.

There it was again – what sounded suspiciously like a gasp and it was coming from his office.

Cautiously he walked back to the office door. He was about to call out again when he heard it. This time he was in no doubt. It was something between a gasp and a whimper, and definitely a sign of pain.

As he entered the room, he stopped in horror.

Mel hung from a noose strung up on one of the exposed beams in the ceiling. Only the contact of her toes with the small bench positioned below stood between her and suffocation. Her hands were behind her back.

"Damien . . ." she gasped, panic in her eyes. "Look –"

He bounded in.

"Stop right there, Flores!"

He halted, his gaze zooming to the source of the barked order. *Alonzo!*

Alonzo stood in the shadows to one side, near the wall-to-wall bookcases. At first glance, everything about him seemed perfectly normal, from the pleasant expression on his face to the casual jeans and t-shirt.

And then he saw the gun in his gloved hand, aimed at him. *His own Glock* pointed directly at him.

He raised the knife and nodded at Mel. "Help me get her down, Alonzo."

Alonzo crowed with laughter. "What are you, a comedian?"

Damien glanced at Mel again, then back at Alonzo. How much longer could she balance on her toes before collapsing? "What are you doing here?" he demanded. "Why have you got my gun?"

Alonzo shook off his laughter. "Forget the chitchat. Drop the knife and kick it towards me."

Damien did as he was told. Heroics were definitely in order, but not just yet.

Alonzo kicked the knife towards the wall. He nodded, then continued as if they were having a casual conversation. "Actually, I got the gun for her." He waved it at Mel. "She's going to kill you, Damien, and then, in remorse, hang herself."

"Yeah?"

"Yeah." He smiled smugly. "Then Cristina will inherit all the Flores money and businesses – that's what it says in the will you signed yesterday. Then I'll marry Cristina, and it will all be mine. Everything you spoiled Flores boys have will finally be mine."

Damien eyed the distance between him and Alonzo. It was about eight feet. If he charged Alonzo, could he disarm him before being killed himself? He tensed in preparation.

"With Cristina being in the detention center, your plans might not work out so well," he said slowly.

Alonzo frowned. "Jail? What are you talking about?"

A choked cry from Mel drew Damien's attention. One of her ankles had given way, and she struggled now to regain her balance on just one foot and relieve the pressure on her throat.

Damien looked hard at Alonzo. "I just came from her place. Cristina's been arrested for sending a threatening letter to Mel and for attempted murder of Joanie. Right about now she's probably spilling her guts to the KWPD about your murder plans."

Alonzo sneered. "Too bad she's not in the loop. She can't spill what she doesn't know. Even if she does go to jail, it won't change anything except the timing. I've waited this long, I can wait a little longer."

He faced Damien directly, the gun pointed at his chest. "Now I just have to decide what's more fun – letting you watch your girlfriend hang and then killing you, or killing you first and then letting su chica die." He extended his arm, racked the slide on the Glock, and smiled.

~ ~ ~

As Mel's toes and leg muscles weakened, the pressure of the rope against her neck grew more intense. Each searing breath was an effort of will, burning her throat and lungs. Her wrists were raw from trying to squeeze her hands free from the plastic cuffs Alonzo had forced onto her.

But the pain in her wrists and lungs was nothing compared to the pain that filled her heart when Damien had barreled into the room.

She'd tried to warn him, but the best she had managed was to croak out his name. Now she was going to have to watch him die – the only man she had ever loved, the only man who had ever loved her.

Then die herself.

She struggled with the cuffs one more time, but it was no use. She doubted her toes would hold her up more than a minute longer. Alonzo wouldn't even have to pull the bench out from under her.

Tears stung her eyes as she thought of all that could have been. Of Kirsten, who would end up in foster care after all. Of Kevin, who would never see his baby.

Then Alonzo did something incredibly thoughtless. He sauntered from his position by the bookcases to one about four feet in front of her. She tensed. This was her chance. *Her only chance.*

Mel teetered backwards on the bench, then swung herself forward and off with all her remaining strength. There was a jarring thud as her foot crashed into Alonzo's elbow. He shrieked as his arm jerked upwards and the gun fired. When Damien launched himself at Alonzo, the two men hit the floor with a crash. Damien went for Alonzo's latex-covered wrist. Mel's surprise attack had given them a chance, but if he didn't get the gun away from Alonzo, it would be game over.

The crack of bone on the floor and Alonzo's howl of pain filled the air as Damien slammed his hand onto the hardwood. As the gun left Alonzo's control, it skidded across the floor and under the large cherry desk.

Fueled by desperation and rage, Alonzo fought like a madman, employing many of the offensive tactics and holds they'd both learned as boys on the wrestling team. But slowly Damien's advanced training as a cop began to win out. He pinned the heaving lawyer to the floor.

Then, with a move Damien didn't anticipate, Alonzo reversed the hold. Howling with rage, his fingers closed around Damien's neck.

Damien grabbed the lawyer's arms and wrenched. Weakened by broken bones, his hold gave way and Damien threw him off. With a surge of adrenalin, he punched Alonzo, sending him crashing headfirst into the bookcases. He slid down, and slumped over onto the floor as a cascade of books fell onto hm. His eyes shut.

Chest heaving, Damien straightened and waited for Alonzo to get up. When he didn't move, he turned to Mel.

~ ~ ~

What he saw sent terror jolting through him. She hung lifeless from the ceiling, her body swinging ever so slightly.

He grabbed the bench, set it upright so he could lift her limp form into his arms. Once the pressure was off the noose, he was able to loosen it, slide it over her head, and lower her to the ground. Her wrists were still cuffed behind her back but that would have to wait.

Her chest didn't move and he couldn't hear any sound of breathing. Blue color tinged her lips and the surrounding skin. Silently praying, he lifted her chin with one hand and pressed her forehead back with the other. He lowered his ear to her mouth. Nothing.

Quickly he lifted her chin with one hand, and pressed back her forehead with the other. He pinched her nose shut with his thumb and index finger and, watching her chest, covered her mouth with his and gave two full breaths.

Her chest rose. He removed his mouth and released her nostrils. He heard the gentle sound of air escaping from her lungs as her chest fell.

He waited a second or two, and repeated the motion. Her chest rose and fell in response, but she didn't start breathing on her own.

In desperation, he carried on. Once, twice, three times. "Come on, Mel," he muttered. "Come *on.*"

After removing his mouth the fifth time, it happened. After her chest fell and the breath he'd given her had been expelled, her chest rose again. On its own. Then fell, and rose again.

"Oh, Mel." He cradled her head in his hands. She started coughing and turned her head to one side. Her eyes fluttered open.

"Damien?"

Her croak was barely decipherable, but to Damien it was the most beautiful sound in the world. "Oh, *mi amor,* tu bien. Thank God, you're okay."

He lowered his lips to her forehead and grazed the damp, pale skin.

She squirmed restlessly beneath him. "I . . . ah . . ."

"Shhh, not now. You don't need to talk. It's okay."

"N-n-no." Suddenly she tensed. Her dazed eyes cleared. "Alonzo? Is he –?"

Damien glanced over at the unmoving form covered in books, then turned back to Mel and kissed her tenderly. "It's all right. He's not going anywhere."

She sighed, and for a moment her eyelids fluttered closed.

They opened again and she smiled up at him. She coughed and tried to clear her throat. "I . . ."

Damien touched her lips with his fingers and shook his head. "Don't talk. I know it hurts."

He pulled his cell out of his pocket, happy to see that it still worked, and called 911 requesting an ambulance and police.

When he turned to her again, she struggled to speak. "I . . . Kevin . . . he didn't kill anyone. It was . . . Alonzo . . . all Alonzo."

Susan Haskell

"Hush. I know. The police are coming now for Alonzo." He didn't know the details, but he knew she was telling the truth.

He stroked her hair back from her face. She blinked, her green eyes dark with pain, then opened her mouth again. "I . . ."

He nuzzled her cheek. "Tell me later."

She shook her head. "No." Then winced at the rasping sound of her own voice.

"I . . . " Her eyes, full of yearning, commanded him to let her speak. "I . . . love . . . you."

The scratchy, gasped out words were music to his battered soul, the love in her eyes telling him everything he wanted to know. His spirits lifted. He smiled. Tomorrow looked brighter than it had for a long time.

"You didn't have to tell me that," he said, shaking his head wryly. "I already knew."

He lowered his lips to hers for another kiss, of love and of life.

Epilogue

"Hey Saunders, get in here."

Even after four months, the rumble of Damien's low, sexy voice over the headphones still set Mel's pulse racing.

"On my way," she said. After a last scan of the room, she skirted the packed dance floor on the way to Damien's office. The loudspeakers blasted out the hypnotic sounds of the latest Latin hit and the smell of sweat, smoke, food and beer filled the air. She loved the sounds, the smells, the taste, the history, everything about Viva Zapata, and was so glad she hadn't been forced to leave.

But more than anything, she loved Viva Zapata's owner. She couldn't wait to see him tonight.

She pushed open the door to his office and stepped inside. She stopped, unprepared for the darkness. Where was —

Suddenly a hand grabbed the front of her shirt. Damien captured her lips in a demanding kiss that sent her into instant meltdown. Her hands went around his neck and she rose on tiptoe to meet his smoldering kiss with one of her own.

After a moment she drew back and nuzzled his rough cheek. "We have to stop meeting like this."

"We could if you'd move back into my house with Kirsten," he growled. His hand slid down her belly and between her legs.

She sighed even as she moved against him. At Damien's request, she'd agreed to keep working at Viva Zapata, but had jumped at Don and Betty Leeson's suggestion she and Kirsten live with them for a few months.

Because no matter how Mel twisted and turned it, Kevin's shadow loomed big between them. It didn't matter that Alonzo Salva had been charged with the murders of Tony, Ryan and Kevin, and with the attempted murder of herself and Damien. It didn't matter that Kevin's role had been to steal Tony's Zuma and shut off the power at Viva Zapata, and that Alonzo had set him up to take the blame. Had Kevin known that Alonzo's plans included killing Tony and Ryan and Damien? She would never know.

Her guilt over not knowing Kevin's role had made her reluctant to return to Damien's arms, but his persistence along with his fairness was slowly winning her over. She could not believe his kindness towards Cristina once he'd realized his sister-in-law had known nothing of Alonzo's murder plans. Cristina was awaiting a hearing now for uttering a death threat, but in the meantime she was working at Blue Heaven, a popular Key West restaurant owned by one of Damien's friends.

Damien rubbed against Mel and kissed her forehead. "Actually, I didn't bring you in here just to ravish you, though that's definitely on the agenda. There's something I want to tell you."

Out of habit, she tensed. "What?"

"Hey, it's good news." He nipped at her ear. "Dan called today."

"And?"

"And the police have arrested a guy for your sister's murder. Name's Al Henderson. Know him?"

"No." Mel could hardly get the word out for the lump in her throat.

"Well, it doesn't matter. The case against him is pretty solid. Apparently he left Key West after Darla's death, but must have thought it was safe to come back."

Mel felt around on the wall for the light switch, and turned it on.

As her eyes adjusted to the light, she looked up at Damien. "How – how did you know about this?"

"Remember that day we went out to Shooters N Scooters? When I made you miss your interview and you told me about your sister? I asked Dan to look up the case. It's not in his area, but he's been keeping an eye on it, calling every once in a while with questions or leads."

"You . . . you did this for me?"

"Yes."

"Why? I mean, after Kevin and . . . and Tony . . ."

Damien traced her lips lightly with one finger. "What's past is past, Mel. Nothing you or I do can bring them back. But there's one thing that I *can* do."

"What's that?"

His eyes, dark and soft as the deepest night, embraced her. If she'd had any doubt just how much he loved her, it was there, in his eyes, clear and bright and burning away the shadows.

"I can make sure every day that you know just how much I love you."

His kiss said the rest.

❄ ❄ ❄

About the Authors

Although fraternal twins born in Canada, Norah-Jean and Susan spent their lives apart.

Susan has lived in Canada and on both US coasts and the Midwest. She was an Operating Nurse assisting in hip replacements to heart surgeries. As a traveler, she has experienced over 50 countries (still more to go). But being a Mum was her favorite job.

Norah-Jean has spent her working life in Ontario, Canada, as a newspaper reporter, freelance writer and editor, and fiction author. She has published five novels, *Outrageous, Blue Dawn, Crazy in Chicago, Alien's Daughter and Night Secrets.* Her inspiration has come from thrills and chills in places as far flung as Timbuktu, West Africa; Sydney, Australia; and down the street from the Shakespeare Festival in Stratford, Ontario. She has a loving husband, and three grown children who keep returning to the "empty nest" despite her best efforts to keep them away.

Fate then brought the girls together again in Key West. Did we mention that Susan is 6 feet tall and Norah-Jean is five feet. tall?

Susan Haskell

ABSOLUTELY AMAZING eBOOKS

AbsolutelyAmazingEbooks.com
or AA-eBooks.com

Made in the USA
Columbia, SC
10 May 2024